I0728069

DO YOU FEAR WHAT I FEAR

~ THE NOEL KRINGLE CHRONICLES ~

REBECCA M. SENESE

ALSO BY REBECCA M. SENESE

The Noel Kringle Chronicles (in reading order)

Santa Claus: Private Detective

Santa Must Die!

The Claus Connection

The Twelve Deaths of Christmas

Baby, It's Deadly Outside

Do You Fear What I Fear

The Man Who Would Be Santa

Who Killed Santa?

The Elf Who Saved Christmas

Wreck the Halls: 5 Christmas Horror Stories

A Very Zombie Christmas

The Santa Murders

DO YOU FEAR WHAT I FEAR

~ THE NOEL KRINGLE CHRONICLES ~

REBECCA M. SENESE

RFAR Publishing
Toronto, Canada

Published 2025 by RFAR Publishing
250A Eglinton Avenue East
Suite 147
Toronto, ON M4P 1K2
Canada
https://www.RFARPublishing.com

This book was manufactured using paper and ink products in accordance with commercial standards.

This is a work of fiction. All characters and events portrayed in this book are fictional, and any resemblance to real people or incidents is purely coincidental.

The author supports the right of humans to control their artistic works. No part of this book has been created using AI-generated images or narrative, as known by the author.

Trade paperback edition, hardcover edition, and electronic editions designed by Rebecca M. Senese / RFAR Publishing in Vellum Press.

2nd Edition Trade Paperback ISBN: 978-1-927603-93-2

RFAR Publishing Trade Paperback 2nd Edition 2025

Printed and bound by IngramSpark.
Australia: Ingram Content Group AU Pty Ltd, Melbourne, Victoria.
US: Lightning Source LLC, La Vergne, Tennessee / Allentown, Pennsylvania / Jackson, Tennessee, United States.
UK: Lightning Source UK Ltd, Milton Keynes, United Kingdom.
Europe: Lightning Source UK Ltd, with facilities in Germany, France, and Spain.

Authorized Representative in the European Economic Area:
Lightning Source France
1 Av. Johannes Gutenberg, 78310
Maurepas, France.
compliance@lightningsource.fr

DEDICATION

For Richard Matheson

DO YOU FEAR WHAT I FEAR

~ THE NOEL KRINGLE CHRONICLES ~

CHAPTER

ONE

The cold October wind ruffled the collar of my navy blue pea coat. The sky was an overcast slate grey, heavy with threatening rain. The air smelled crisp and cool, with a tinge of earthiness. The grass under my feet was still dark green, as if remembering the summer that was now at least a month and a half away.

Around me, tombstones and monuments sprouted out of the ground. Most looked worn and dull. Several were cracked with moss growing along the sides, even obscuring the inscriptions.

I shifted a little to the left, adjusting my hands in the pockets of my coat. As I moved, I could feel my left leg bump into something. I glanced over. A dark grey tombstone tilted away from me.

"Sorry about that," I said.

"Don't worry about it," said Cameron Rogers. "It actually looks better a little crooked like that."

The man stepped past me and reached for the tombstone. He grabbed hold of it with two hands and tilted it a little farther.

"There, that's even better," he said.

We stood in the middle of Cameron's large, L-shaped lawn which was decorated like a cemetery. It was the most elaborately decorated lawn I had ever seen for Halloween.

Not that I had seen very many Halloween decorations.

Halloween was never a big thing up at the North Pole. But since I had moved down to Toronto to be a private detective, Halloween had become my favourite time of year.

Well, second favourite.

I had to stay loyal to Dad. After all, not every one had a real life icon for a father. But being Noel Kringle, youngest son of Kris and Mary Kringle, had its burdens as well.

One of those burdens was my older brother Kris Junior, who went as KJ.

KJ took Christmas very seriously and although he had come to have some respect for what I did, it was very begrudging and he never could bring himself to understand why I had left the North Pole.

But, as being the youngest son of Kris Kringle meant I would never take over the job of Santa Claus, I had decided to leave the North Pole to come to Toronto to be a private detective.

And had managed to make a go of it. Even if the occasional case did turn out to be somewhat odd.

Maybe some.

Okay, maybe most of them. But not all.

Definitely not all.

But the issue Cameron Rogers was having was probably a simple act of vandalism. After all, kids were always looking to cause mischief around Halloween and Halloween decorations. Especially elaborate ones like Cameron put up.

Cameron's large, two-storey, dark red brick house was situated on a corner lot and he used the entire length of his L-shaped lawn for his cemetery. Black iron bars with pointed spikes on top separated the cemetery from the sidewalk. Even as we stood in the middle of the lawn at four-thirty on a Sunday afternoon, people were walking by to take a look or snap photos.

Cameron waved at a family who stood on the other side of the fence.

"Come back at the end of the week when it's finished," he said.

Finished?

It looked more than finished to me. I could easily count ten tombstones around me, and there were probably at least another ten on the longer side of the lawn.

In front of me, closer to the stone porch that curved around the house, stood a six and a half foot zombie.

It was stationary, arms raised half reaching toward me, hands curled into claws. It wore a dark suit, stained with dirt. The sleeves ended in ragged rips. The lapels were torn. Under the jacket, the white shirt had brownish stains.

Probably dirt, I told myself.

What was I thinking? Of course it was dirt, or paint, or something like that. It wouldn't be blood. Not real blood anyway. It was a prop, a fake, even though the zombie face looked frighteningly real.

Even the eyes seemed to almost follow me as I shifted back to my right.

Then the light on the side of the house blinked on, chasing the shadows across the zombie's greenish skin and I realized I was just seeing reflections in its unblinking, marble eyes.

Unnerving though.

I turned to Cameron who stood behind me, making slight adjustments to the tombstone.

The light from the porch highlighted the salt in the salt-and-pepper look of his brown hair. A slight frown crept across his face as he tilted his head to study the tombstone. Tiny crinkles creased the corners of his eyes. Even in this cold, late afternoon, he wore his dark green hoodie unzipped. Frayed jeans covered his legs. His off-white runners had grass stains.

He reached for the tombstone again and from what I could tell, didn't move it at all, but it must have moved a fraction of an inch because this time he stepped back and smiled.

"That's better."

From what I knew of the man, he would continue on like this if I didn't interrupt him.

"So was this the zombie they moved?" I asked.

I jerked my thumb behind me at the reaching, business suit-clad zombie.

"Yeah, that's the one." Cameron stepped around me. "I always have Boris beside the stairs to the front door. But not too close. I don't wanna scare the real young ones. C'mon, I'll show you."

He bounded off, weaving between the tombstones and monuments as he headed around toward the front of the house.

I hurried to catch up.

The grass crunched under my feet. Light from the side porch light cast long shadows that stretched in front of me. If Boris the zombie had been standing at the proper angle, I was sure his shadow would have been reaching for me.

I shivered in the cool air from the thrill of it.

There was something delightful about a holiday designed to scare you. It was so different from Christmas.

Which was why I hadn't been too sure about the job when Cameron Rogers had shown up in my office just a few days ago.

He had called ahead of time to schedule an appointment about a vandalism case. Venir, one of my associates, and an ex-Christmas Elf with a voice gruffer than any I'd ever heard, had set up the appointment.

It had been a surprise, since Venir had started to lobby for me to hire a receptionist.

"Kid, you gotta get some staff," he'd told me, rolling an unlit cigar between the fingers of his left hand. Rolling the cigar was the only thing I let him do in the office. I would not allow him to smoke.

"I don't earn enough for staff," I said.

But as usual, that wouldn't deter Venir for long. Before he could gather himself for another assault, the door to the waiting room creaked open.

Venir vanished in what I called a *wink* because it took about as fast as a wink to disappear.

Leaving me to answer the door. Just to illustrate his point that we needed a receptionist.

Which we did not, especially since there was nowhere to put one.

When I stepped out of my small office, I found myself facing a man dressed in a tailored suit and a beige, camel-hair coat.

"Are you Noel Kringle?" he asked. "Of SC Investigations?"

"Yes, I am," I said. "Can I help you mister...?"

"Rogers, Cameron Rogers. I made an appointment with your assistant."

"Right, come on in."

I led the way back through into my small office. There was barely enough room in front of my desk for two hard-backed chairs. I squeezed around the right end of my metal desk, bought used at Goodwill, and sat down in my creaking leather chair.

I had my laptop on the left side of my burgundy desk blotter and a scattering of standard desk accoutrements along the top. Contrary to appearance, they were anything but standard. My mother had taken it upon herself to send along a stapler, a charcoal-coloured cup for pens, a paper clip holder that swirled with etched snowflakes, a silver letter opener with more snowflakes curling up the silver blade and my name carved into the wooden handle, and a very special leather notebook that magically copied everything I wrote in it into the proper computer file for that case, as well as into my paper files, and then erased itself whenever the case was completed.

Although they looked like normal desk items, each had their own magic woven into them.

To round out the look of my private detective office, I kept my favourite hat, a dark, charcoal grey Stingy Brim – think fedora but with a smaller brim – on the right side of my desk.

If the man in the tailored suit looked down on my tiny office, I could see no indication as he sat on the chair in front of my desk.

"You're looking for a private detective, Mr. Rogers," I said.

"That's right," he said. "I'd like to keep it quiet if possible. I have some very nervous partners."

"You can count on my discretion," I said. "Tell me your problem."

"Well, as I mentioned to your assistant, it's a vandalism problem at my home haunt."

I blinked and leaned forward. "Excuse me?"

"I run a home haunt," he said in a rush. "All through October. I decorate my yard as a cemetery and have a haunted house on my driveway. I raise funds for the CHH, the Children's Healing Hospital. I've been doing it for almost fifteen years and raised over a hundred grand for them."

That took me aback. I had been picturing a tiny, cheezily decorated lawn with inflatable ghosts and cardboard gravestones. But no one would do that for fifteen years or be able to raise that kind of money doing it.

"What's been happening?" I asked.

"Just before Thanksgiving, my crew and I built the haunted house on the driveway and put up most of the cemetery. I take the Thanksgiving weekend off with my family and then continue working on the décor until the week before Halloween, when we open. But I noticed when I went back into the cemetery some things are moved around." He frowned. "We put a lot of work into this and it does a lot of good. I hate to think someone is trying to mess with that."

"Don't worry, we'll find out what's happening and put a stop to it," I said. "Why don't I come and take a look?"

"Okay," he said. "Sunday is best. We'll have more of it done so you can see more of what it's supposed to look like."

"Great," I said. "Give me the address."

AND THAT WAS HOW I'D ENDED UP FACE TO FACE WITH TOMBSTONES and zombies on a late Sunday afternoon a week before Halloween.

"Over here," Cameron called. He stood near the bottom of the stairs leading to his front porch. Tucked into the side of the stairs was a large bush, still full of leaves.

"That's where I put Boris," Cameron said.

He pointed to an empty spot behind the bush. I stepped closer. The grass was sparse there. Even in the shadows, I could see the ground was scraped. If Boris the zombie had been placed here, someone had dragged it out.

Although if I squinted and looked at the scratches a little differently in the dirt, I could almost imagine Boris dragging his heels as he shuffled out of his hiding spot, looking to attack any unwary travelers.

I shook my head. Too much imagination.

I stood up and turned back toward Cameron. From my spot near where Boris had been, I could see how it was a good spot for the zombie. Mostly hidden by the bush, the littler children wouldn't be able to see the big zombie looming up above the leaves. But taller kids or adults would be able to see it.

A bit of a thrill for them.

"Good spot," I said.

"Yeah, isn't it?" he said. "See, I got Karloff over on the other side of the stairs."

He pointed. I pushed past the bush to meet him at the fence that separated us from the concrete path leading to the stairs.

Sure enough, across the way, peering out of a matching bush, I spotted the pale face of a vampire. The mouth was open, revealing sharp fangs. Blood was smeared across the lower lip and down the chin. White, pointed ears curved up on the sides of the vampire's head, poking out from underneath the black hair.

I tilted my head.

Those ears...

They looked remarkably like Venir's, although Venir's ears curved up over the top of his head and poked through the mass of curling white hair on the Elf's head.

I pressed my lips tight together to stop the chuckle. I was *not* going to tell Venir about this resemblance. He wouldn't appreciate it.

But I sure did.

"So they didn't bother the vampire," I said. "Karloff is an odd name for a vampire."

"It goes with Boris," Cameron said.

He looked at me expectantly. I shrugged, feeling the scratch of my coat collar against my cheek. Fortunately most of my cheek was still bare. My dark brown beard grew along my jaw line until mid-November, then as Christmas grew closer, my beard would grow longer and busier, draining of colour until it was snow white.

My hair did the same thing.

One of the perks of being Santa Claus's son. Along with my magic, although that was massively curtailed away from the North Pole.

But for now, I was as safe as I was for most of the year with my mass of brown wavy hair and neatly trimmed, brown beard.

"Boris Karloff," Cameron said. "He was a famous horror movie star. Just like Bela Legosi, Christopher Lee, Peter Cushing."

He paused, probably waiting for me to recognize the names.

But horror movies had never been big at the North Pole.

"Sorry," I said. "I don't know them."

Cameron shook his head. "They're classics. Let me grab you some DVDs before you go."

Before I could stop him, he spun away from me and bounded back toward the side of the lawn.

I realized I might have to sit on him. There was no other way I could get him to stay still long enough to tell me what was going on.

But clearly something was. Someone had gotten into his display and moved Boris the zombie from beside the stairs all the way around the side of the house.

Unless Boris had come alive and dragged his shoddy carcass over there himself.

I chuckled. Then my chuckle died in the cold air.

That couldn't possibly happen.

Could it?

"Here you go, check these out." Cameron appeared from the side of the house and shoved a stack of DVD cases into my hands.

"You've got Dracula. Classic right there. Bride of Frankenstein. Even though it's the sequel it's way better than the original. They were still figuring out how movies should look at that point. Then this one is the best Christopher Lee in my opinion. And this one is great Peter Cushing, although he's the villain in this one. He usually plays Van Helsing to Lee's Dracula."

"These are all great, Cameron," I said. "But I'm here to find out about the vandalism."

"Right. Of course you are." He glanced around as if waking from a dream.

"So Boris should be there behind the bush, but he was around the side where I showed you. And several of the tombstones were disturbed. I'll show you."

He took a step close to the fence. With a flick of his hand, he pushed forward and an entire section swung away. I followed him, carrying the DVDs under my arm.

We crossed the walk and into the other section of the lawn. Cameron showed me the tombstones that had been moved. Instead of being scattered around the space, they had been lined up close together, as if making a small wall.

"See, it ruins the aesthetic," Cameron said.

Never having thought about the aesthetic of a fake cemetery, I could only nod in sympathy.

"Do you have security cameras?" I asked.

"Sure do." He pointed toward the house.

I peered closer. Nestled against the brick, I spotted two small cameras pointed down.

"Got two others along the side," Cameron said. "But they don't show anything. The feed goes all staticy. They must have a way to interfere with it."

I nodded. "I'll check that out. In the meantime, myself or one of my associates will stake out the house and make sure no one interferes with your cemetery tonight."

"You really think that'll work?" he asked. "Won't whoever is doing this see you hanging around?"

"Don't worry, Mr. Rogers, they won't see a thing. I guarantee it."

CHAPTER

TWO

After promising Cameron I would be sure to watch some of the DVDs he'd given me, I returned to my office. Out of sight of Cameron's home or any watching neighbours, I *winked* back, landing in my office chair.

With Venir's help, I had learned to stretch my meagre magic by learning to anchor several locations in the city into my mind so I could *wink* to them using as little magic as possible. One of those locations was my office, and specifically my office chair.

But to actually land in it and not be displaced into the waiting room was a real treat. Too many times, Venir would be sitting in my chair when I tried to *wink* into it. No matter how many times I asked, he always snuck in to sit behind my desk.

The WiFi was better there, he'd say, or the light was better, or the air, or whatever. Any excuse to sit behind my desk. But I knew the real reason.

Just like lobbying for a receptionist, Venir had become convinced that he should have his own office with his own desk.

Because he'd worked with me on several cases, he seemed to think I was somehow swimming in money and should be able to afford a luxurious office and lots of staff.

But as he'd never had to pay rent or food costs, he didn't really understand about money.

So since he couldn't have his own office, like he believed he was entitled to, he often commandeered mine when I wasn't around.

Hence it being nice to be able to land in my own chair rather than be displaced into the waiting room.

I breathed in the office air. After the crisp, coldness of Cameron's front lawn, my office smelled a little stale. I spun my chair so I faced the window behind my desk. In the summer, I had an air conditioner stuck in there but with the cooling temperatures of fall, I had pulled it out and stuck it under the far corner of my desk.

I had only stubbed a toe on it once.

No, twice.

I pulled the Venetian blinds up and cracked the window open. Cool air drifted in, smelling of dust and asphalt, carried up from the empty, gravel parking lot that stretched out beyond my window. When I had rented this office, sight unseen, from the North Pole, the landlord had assured me of a lake front view.

He hadn't bothered to mention the lake could only be viewed from the other side of the building, and only if you manage to peer through a window at one end.

But now I didn't mind. I had come to accept the view of the unused lot beyond and the three crumbling, deserted warehouses that sat across the way. Contemplating their slowly sagging roofs had often helped clear my mind.

It was just too bad that the air wasn't quite as crisp and clean as at Cameron's house.

I turned back to my desk. Who could I assign to watch Cameron's front yard? Venir was probably the most inconspicuous of us but he had been quite demanding lately. If I gave him another assignment he would probably use it as leverage in his bid to get me to hire a receptionist.

Maybe I'd hold off on using him.

Then there was Palle.

Somehow I didn't see Palle being inconspicuous at all.

In his natural form as a troll, Palle was almost nine feet tall with pale green skin, tusks that protruded from the sides of his mouth, and long, pointed ears that rose above his bald head. When he smiled, he looked like he was angry enough to tear your head off, but I had come to know the gentle soul that resided in that scary-looking, huge body.

Thanks to a masking spell, Palle could hide his troll self behind the image of a large, burly man with scruffy brown hair. But even in that guise he was still noticeable.

That only left one option.

Me.

I was going to have to fortify myself with coffee before I reported for duty at Cameron's house. And I was also going to have to check on one more aspect that concerned me.

The cameras.

I didn't know enough about home security systems but there was someone I could ask.

She answered the phone on the second ring with her customary, curt response, "Talk ta me."

"Hi Shirl, it's Noel. Do you know anything about home security systems?"

She snorted. "WiFi connected, 'course."

"Is there a way to interfere with the cameras to cause static on the recording?"

"I'm gonna have to look into that," she said. "My usual rate."

Her usual rate was a lot more than mine. "Look for an hour and then get back to me," I said.

She grunted agreement and hung up.

Shirl Trombley was a hacker that I had met through a detective and had become my defacto computer expert. Even though I had helped rescue her nephew from a twenty year curse, and restored her memory of him, she still charged me her regular rate.

Sort of. I wasn't sure but I didn't think she ever charged me for all of her hours. And she'd stopped complaining about how long it took me to pay her.

For now at least.

With that sorted, there was one other avenue I could look into before I headed back to Cameron's house.

I tightened my red scarf around my neck and made sure my hat was securely on my head. Then I buttoned my coat over blue flannel shirt and dark blue jeans before I gathered myself and *winked.*

I landed several feet back from the mouth of an alley off Yonge Street. Any hint of sunshine was gone, disappearing behind the heavy clouds and the night sky. It was barely five o'clock and it looked like midnight.

I'd heard lots of people complain about that since I'd come to Toronto but I'd kept my mouth shut. After living with six months of darkness at the North Pole followed by six months of blinding sunshine, having any kind of regular day and night schedule felt like a luxury.

A cool breeze from the alley behind me carried the stale remnants of rotting vegetables and burned baked goods. Discarded newspapers crackled under my feet as I headed toward the street.

Even for a Sunday, Yonge Street was somewhat busy with cars. The sidewalk was alight with blazing store signs and streetlights that turned the late afternoon darkness into day. But as I strolled past clothing shops I noticed the cashiers starting to close up.

That was a potentially bad sign. I might be too late after all.

I hurried on until I came to the place I was looking for.

The delicatessen was tucked into a narrow space with barely enough room for the glass door. I pulled it open and the rich smells of corned beef and the yeasty odour of fresh bread filled my nostrils, driving out the last of the rotting vegetables.

I inhaled and my mouth instantly started watering. I'd been thinking I could use a sandwich as a bribe but now that I was here I was going to get myself something as well. With a long night ahead of me, I would need my own fortification.

I stepped up to the glass counter. The short, wizened-looking woman behind it smirked at me as she tugged at the front of her hairnet. She wore an apron stained with ketchup on the front. Plastic gloves covered her hands. She looked like some cheap, black-market surgeon.

"Detective Stan," she croaked.

"Right," I said. "And I'll take a ham and cheese on brown roll."

She gave me a thumbs up and got to work.

She plunked two thick slices of rye bread in the toaster then sliced up a brown roll and tossed it onto a conveyor belt that slowly churned constantly into an oven that toasted items that were too thick for the toaster. While the bread and bun were toasting, she assembled Detective Stan Mallory's favourite sandwich on a sheet of wax paper. Wafer thin slices of roast beef, topped with three slices of Swiss cheese. A generous swirl of mustard topped it off. For mine, she piled slices of ham high before covering it with a thick slice of cheddar.

She lifted the mustard and cocked an eyebrow at me.

"For you?" she asked.

"Just mayo," I said.

She gave a curt nod before grabbing the toasted bread and bun and finishing the sandwiches. As the wax paper crackled while she wrapped them, I moved down the counter to the cash register where a young woman stood. She wore a matching apron to the old woman except hers was clean and her black hair was piled up on her head in a mass of curls.

As I reached the cashier, the old woman barked a guttural sounding word. The young woman paused and shot me an inquisitive look, then she responded to the old woman with a few clipped words. The old woman shook her head and repeated her guttural word. The young woman shrugged.

"Five dollars," she said to me.

I had already pulled out a twenty. "Excuse me?"

"Five dollars." She tilted her head an inch toward the old woman. The old woman nodded at me with an expression that said she would not brook any dissension.

But my mother would never have let me take advantage of someone like this. I started to hand the twenty over to the cashier but the old woman clapped her hands. The plastic muffled the sound but it still thumped across the counter.

"Papa Santa," the old woman said.

I froze and looked over at her. She gave me another curt nod. A smile curled the corners of her lips.

Had she heard my name and realized who I was?

Everyone else who heard my name just thought it was a gimmick, a coincidence, or an odd choice. No one ever thought it was real, not unless I told them and proved it.

But the knowledge seemed to shine out of the old woman's eyes. Or at least a strong suspicion. Maybe that was enough for her, but I still couldn't let her give me my food for free.

I leaned over to the cashier. "Can you tell her that it would be a gift to me to allow me to pay for my sandwich?"

The woman repeated the message. A frown creased the old woman's face.

"Santa doesn't do it for a reward," I said. "He prefers to give without expectation."

The frown faded from the old woman's face. The lines in her skin smoothed out and for a moment, I caught a glimpse of the young girl within. Immediately, her favourite Christmas gift flooded into my mind, a handmade doll given to her by her grandmother.

I yanked my gaze away from her before the details could solidify in my mind. A woman who had guessed my identity could probably feel the magic tingling in the air.

When I shoved the twenty dollars toward the cashier this time, she took it. As she made change, I pressed my hands against the counter, trying to stop them from trembling from the magical buildup I could feel in my mind. Once an image of someone's favourite Christmas gift started in my mind, it almost felt like a magical compulsion to see all of it.

I couldn't let it happen this time. Not in front of that old woman.

But it was already too late. As I took the change and the bag with the sandwiches from the cashier, the old woman leaned over the glass counter. She must have crawled onto a chair to do it. As I turned and walked by, she leaned farther over.

"Eat well, Santa's boy," her voice whispered as I passed her.

I could feel my cheeks redden. She leaned away and cackled a loud laugh.

So much for fooling her.

I pushed the door open and stepped out into the cold early evening air.

Next stop, the precinct and the small, dingy cubicle of Detective Stan Mallory.

CHAPTER

THREE

The front sergeant wasn't someone I knew but he recognized the bag I carried and was willing to call the detective squad. From the way he eyed the bag, maybe he thought I would give him the sandwich if Mallory wasn't around. The hopeful gleam died as he hung up the phone.

"Through there and then follow the…"

"Yes, I know the way," I said.

I could feel his gaze on the bag as I headed around the end of the counter and through the metal detector.

Stan Mallory's cubicle was a small, grey cubby in the centre of a mass of grey cubicles. At the very least they weren't the same fading mint green colour as the walls.

When I entered the room of cubicles, blinding fluorescent lights blazed forth. In the distant corner on the right, one of the lights sputtered, creating a staccato rhythmic pattern that would have driven any normal person mad. But here in the detective squad, they probably didn't even notice.

When I reached Mallory's cubicle, I crinkled the paper bag before I poked my head through the cubicle opening. After a moment, I did so and found Mallory sitting bolt upright in his chair, eyes wide with interest.

"Is that...?" he asked.

"It is," I said and set the paper bag down on his desk.

It took him a fraction of a second to claim his sandwich and take a bite. He gave a grunt of approval as he chewed. A serene look of satisfaction spread across his face. It was as close to contentment as I'd ever seen on him.

I had met Stan Mallory during my first case when I'd been arrested on suspicion of murder. Knowing his favourite Christmas gift had gotten me out of jail and giving it back to him had gotten his help in stopping a rogue goblin. Only then had he really believed my story of being Kris Kringle's youngest son.

Since then, Mallory was not only a useful contact to have in the police department, he had become a friend. One I didn't at all mind treating to his favourite sandwich.

By the time I'd managed two bites of my ham and cheddar cheese sandwich, Mallory was halfway finished his. He slowed down enough to focus on me.

"So, what's the favour?" he asked before taking another bite.

I chewed, enjoying the crisp, toasted bread. Then I swallowed and patted my mouth with a napkin.

"Who says I have a favour to ask?" I said.

"You always have a favour to ask," he said. He gave an exaggerated grump at the end but I knew him well enough now to know when he was just acting annoyed rather than actually *being* annoyed.

"Maybe I'm just here to see your smiling face," I said. "Or bask in your sparkling personality."

Mallory narrowed his eyes at me. "I can totally see why your brother hates you."

I laughed. KJ and I had our differences but I didn't think he actually hated me.

Then my laughter slowed. At least I didn't think he did.

I stopped laughing and glared at Mallory.

He tried to look innocent but it's difficult with graying hair buzzed short above a wide, weathered face that looked like it had taken less punches that he had given. He wore his customary white shirt with the sleeves rolled up to his elbows. His forearms were thick and strong looking, with faint grey hairs sprouting out of them.

"Okay, I have a favour to ask," I said. "Do you know of any kids doing vandalism up around the Woodcrest area?"

"Woodcrest? That's mostly suburbs up there. What kind of thing are you looking for?"

I hesitated. How could I explain it and not make it sound cheesy the way I had assumed it was?

"Well, it's vandalism of a Halloween display," I said. "The

owner raises money for the Children's Healing Hospital and he does an elaborate display..."

"Wait a minute," Mallory interrupted. "Are you talking about the Woodcrest Haunted House?"

I blinked at the excitement in his voice. "You've heard of it?"

"Of course, the guy's been running it for years. He goes on the local stations during their Halloween broadcasts. He even has to hire off duty officers to deal with the traffic."

"He does?" I asked.

"Oh sure. One of the guys said there was close to four thousand people there last Halloween."

I almost dropped the sandwich. "Are you kidding me?"

"Nope, almost four thousand people. He had more the year before, I heard, when it wasn't raining."

I took a bite of my sandwich and chewed mechanically. The texture of the ham and cheese lost its flavour as I focused on what Mallory was telling me.

And what Cameron Rogers hadn't.

Had he omitted it on purpose or had it just slipped his mind? He didn't seem like the kind of man who would forget something like that. But I had only met him a couple of times. What did I really know about him?

I knew he spent a lot of money and time to celebrate a holiday and to raise money for a worthy cause. That afforded him some leeway.

"So wait, are you telling me someone is vandalizing his haunted house?" Mallory asked.

His voice started to rise in indignation. Anger darkened his features.

I could just imagine what he would do if he got his hands on any teenage kids I suspected were doing it.

"I don't know what's happening," I said. "Some of the props in the cemetery have been moved around. It's probably just kids pulling pranks. I'm staking out the house tonight to keep an eye on it."

Mallory's frown deepened. "Doesn't he have a security system? He should."

"Yes, but it's just showing static. I've got Shirl looking into it," I said. "Meanwhile, I'm going to stake it out overnight."

Mallory swept the wax paper sheet and the empty paper bag off his desk with one sweep of his arm. He crumbled them together into a tiny ball and tossed them into the bin under his desk.

"Finish up and we'll go," he said.

"What?" I said. "I just wanted to know if there had been any vandalism in the area."

"Right. I can check on that now."

He turned back to his computer, an old, black desktop that whined when he started typing into it. He clicked through several screens, did a little more typing, a little more clicking, and then stopped.

"Nothing reported," he said. He rolled his chair back, putting his hands on the armrests, preparing to rise. "Finish up and let's go."

"Stan, this is my case," I said. "It's just an overnight stake out. I don't need you..."

"You didn't ask," he said. "I'm telling you. I'm coming with you. You got a problem with that?"

He glared across the desk from me. Now I could tell that he was annoyed with me.

"No, no problem," I said and took a huge bite of my sandwich.

Under Mallory's watchful glare, I forced myself to eat the remaining half of it barely managing to chew or taste any of it.

Finally, I tossed the final mouthful into my mouth. Mallory snatched up the wax paper, crumpled it and tossed it out.

"Let's go," he said.

"Yes, sir," I said.

What else do you say to a man who's armed?

By the time we returned to Cameron Rogers's house on the corner of Woodcrest, the sun had disappeared completely. There was no hint of light behind the thick layer of clouds in the sky. The street lights were on, casting pools of yellowish light against the encroaching darkness.

Mallory drove his car past the house once. In full darkness with only the pale streetlights, the cemetery looked even more real. The shadows were thicker. The tombstones looked like real stone. I could almost smell the moss through the closed windows and had to remind myself that even it was fake.

Other figures loomed in the darkness of the cemetery. Boris was still on the side of the cemetery. Cameron hadn't moved him back to his spot beside the stairs yet. At the far end of the front, I spotted a grave digger in a long, brown coat. He held a shovel in one hand and the hair of a dangling severed head in the other. Long blond hair spilled over the shoulders of the figure. A wide brimmed hat covered the face in shadow but I could swear I saw the eyes catch a glint of light from the street lights.

Not even finished, I remember Cameron saying. What was this place going to look like when it *was* finished?

Spectacular enough to draw a crowd of thousands.

And the mischievousness of a few troublemakers.

When we finished the drive by, Mallory parked the car on the side street just across from the house, in between two street lights. The pool of darkness seemed the perfect size to cover the car and hide us within it.

From the windshield, we could see the whole front of Cameron's house but none of the side.

"What about the side?" I asked Mallory.

He turned off the car. Light from the headlights vanished, shrouding us in darkness. I could still make out his shrug in the gloom.

"This is the best I can do and keep out of sight of the house," he said. "We don't want the vandals spotting us. I suppose you would have parked right on the same street near the corner so you could see the whole lawn."

Sarcasm dripped from his voice.

He seemed to be forgetting who he was talking to. It might be a good time to remind him.

"I wouldn't need a car," I said, my voice low and casual. "I would be waiting in the middle of the display and they would never see me."

Silence from the other side of the car.

I waited for his response. Was he going to kick me out of the car?

"Right," he said. "Sorry. I suppose I should have... well, sorry."

"I know what I'm doing, Stan," I said.

"I know you do, Noel. Really, I'm sorry. And I'm sorry about the crack about your brother earlier. That was uncalled for. You probably *could* do a better job of staking out the place on your own. Maybe I should leave you to it."

He sounded genuinely sorry.

I definitely had made my point, maybe a little stronger than I needed to. He really seemed to want to be here. He'd known all about the haunted house Cameron ran and it seemed to be important to him.

"No, you don't have to leave," I said.

"Great," he said. "You take the first watch. Wake me in four hours and we'll switch."

I heard a click and then a thump as his seat flopped back. A few moments later, soft snores sounded from his side of the car.

Genuinely sorry.

Right.

I'd been played by a master.

CHAPTER

FOUR

I spent the first few hours listening to Mallory's increasingly loud snores while watching the front lawn of Cameron's house. From our position, parked down the street that angled away from the front, I could see the entire lawn to the left end of his house where a large tree grew. In the yellowish glow from the street light, its empty branches waved from side to side, casting dancing shadows on the front porch.

The temperature was dropping in the car. It had to be at least five degrees colder outside, maybe ten. Would any vandal come out in this chill?

I hoped to find out.

I assumed they would head into the front portion of the lawn but if they stayed on the right side, I would never see them from here.

I tapped my fingers on the brim of my hat as it rested in my lap. If I had staked out the house on my own, a simple spell could have kept me hidden from view, just out of eyesight. I knew one from Dad. He used it avoid any children trying to spy on him while he delivered toys on Christmas Eve. It entailed just staying out of eyeshot, out of the corner of someone's eye. It didn't make you invisible but it did make it impossible for someone else to see you if they tried.

It took a little effort to pull off and maintain. I had planned to start it in my office and then *wink* here but Mallory's insistence on coming with me had stopped that.

I didn't have all the ingredients with me. I could try *winking* to my office and back but for that time, the house would be unobserved. If someone came along then, I'd never know.

Leaving my post was not an option. I was not going to squelch on my duty. Doing my duty had been drummed into me practically from birth.

Maybe there was a slight variation I could do on the spell, something that was temporary. Long enough that I could slip out of the car and check on the other side of the display.

Many spells had that, a less powerful version. I'd never tried with this distraction spell but it might work.

The one thing I did wish I had was a focus point. Preferably one that was magically charged. I knew the perfect item. A cane I had brought with me from the Magical Realms when I'd helped stop a rogue faerie bent on disrupting the peace between the Summer and Winter Courts, a peace my father just happened to have brokered. It had originally been a staff but before I'd crossed back in to the Human Realm, I had used blood magic to bind it to me and condense it down from the tall staff it had originally been to a regular sized cane of black polished wood. I kept it in the bottom drawer of my desk, a drawer I had enchanted to hold magical items and to hide them from anyone looking for them.

That cane would have been the perfect focal point and a perfect support for the spell.

Too bad I didn't have it with me.

So what could I use?

I felt my fingers tighten on the brim of my hat.

My hat.

Well, why not? I rather liked it, so why not infuse it with a little magic? Maybe that way it wouldn't ever get blown off my head.

Worth a shot.

But I would have to cast the spell outside of the car. I couldn't risk Mallory being affected by it, especially since I wasn't quite sure how doing a truncated version of it would turn out.

I glanced up and down the street. Everything was still and quiet. Lights still burned in the windows of a few of the houses, but as the hours had passed, more and more of them had blinked off. It was almost like the houses were closing their eyes. Even as I grabbed the car handle and pushed the door open, another house across the road fell into darkness as its lights switched off.

I stepped out of the car onto the asphalt of the street. Chill air caressed my cheek. I closed the door behind me with a soft click.

I breathed deeply, filling my lungs with the sharp tang of earth and hint of dust. Two steps and I stood in the middle of the road.

I set my hat down and knelt in front of it. Another deep breath and I could feel myself sinking into a trance. The air around me cooled further. I closed my eyes.

The words of the spell rose in my mind. At times, it felt like magic was a creature with its own mind that wished to be unleashed. At other times, it felt like a muscle I had to work on.

Tonight it felt like a curtain that wanted to wrap around me. Or maybe that's how I envisioned the spell.

The moment I thought about it, I could feel my magic swirling around me, as if seeking out the ingredients to manifest itself forth. Too bad I didn't have them all.

Instead, I brought my attention to my hat. The Stingy Brim had been with me through a few cases. Although it seemed very cliché, I liked the look of it, how it made me feel like I was in a Raymond Chandler novel or maybe a Mickey Spillane, although I wasn't big on punching people out. And Toronto didn't seem to have too many mean streets.

Especially not a street like Woodcrest.

I brought my attention back to the hat. It was dark grey

with a wide ribbon around it. The narrow brim was the perfect look for me. It went well with my navy pea coat and I was sure it would go well with the black cane.

Even with my eyes closed, I could feel the shift of magic around me.

And the echo of a response.

What? How?

I could feel the cane resonate. But that shouldn't be possible. It was locked in my magically protected drawer. Nothing should be able to affect it.

Except I had bound it to me by blood, and I really wanted it here to help with the spell.

And the cane was answering me.

Was it possible, could I actually call it to me from the drawer?

My heart began to pounded. I took a steadying breath, willing it to settle down. Getting excited didn't help with magic. You had to be calm, collected.

Focused.

I relaxed my shoulders and held my hands in my lap, open, facing up. If I was able to call the cane to myself, I wanted it to show up in my hands, lying across my lap. I thought about the look of it, the smooth black surface, the curl of the handle.

I could almost hear a distant quivering response.

I stayed focused.

Think about the weight of it in my hands. How the

handle would feel in my palm when I flipped it to rest on the ground. The support of it if I put my weight on it.

The air felt charged around me. I smelled ozone. A slight burning stench, like the aftermath of a blown out match. Magic crackled around me. Crackled in my mind.

Something cool and heavy pressed against my open palms but it still felt insubstantial. A promise but not yet a reality.

I took another breath. Focused.

Cane in the drawer. Come to me. *Now!*

I felt the press of solid wood in my hands. I curled my fingers around it, felt the smooth wood.

I opened my eyes.

The black cane lay across my hands.

I could feel the restrained magic potential within it, even in this non-magical realm. I would have to be really careful with it. It had the potential to cause great havoc if I didn't keep a tight rein on its magical properties but I could definitely use it to enhance this spell.

From the way it vibrated in my hands, I could tell that it would do more than just enhance this spell. It could allow me to tap into greater magic than I had access to in Toronto. Ever since I'd left the North Pole, my abilities and my access to magic had been severely restricted. Having more magic at my disposal could be a wonderful thing.

Or it could be disastrous.

In this realm, there was always the danger of unrestrained magic getting unleashed. The havoc that would cause could be immense. I always tried to use as little as possible, not just because I didn't have a lot but because of the effects it might have around me.

Now this cane was offering me more.

No, give me only what I need and no more.

I could feel my command sink deep into the cane. Its resonance changed. It bent itself to my will.

I recited the commands for the spell of distraction and I could feel the air shift around me. The street lights seemed to dim, like their light was no longer on the same frequency as I was.

They probably weren't.

Using the cane, I pushed myself to my feet and swiped up my hat. I placed it on my head and turned toward the house.

The red bricks looked deeper, darker, blending almost into black. As I moved forward, I noticed that even the lawn looked darker. All the colours were darker, like any brightness had been striped from them. I felt like I was encased in shadow.

I probably was. It was probably part of the spell.

Was this how it was for Dad all night long on Christmas Eve? I would have to ask him some time.

I reached the sidewalk and turned right, following the iron fence. My footsteps were silent on the concrete. Interesting how the spell even displaced sound but it made sense. You didn't want to be out of sight but have the noise you made still audible.

I reached the corner and turned.

To see the full view of the side of the cemetery.

And the group of three boys who were standing in front of Boris.

Just as I'd suspected, they'd come back to mess with the static zombie.

All three were dressed in dark hoodies and blue jeans. Two had the hoods pulled up around their faces but the third had his thrown back, revealing long, brown hair hanging in tangled waves around his head.

He was facing away from me, but when he turned toward the boy on his right, I caught a glimpse of profile. A narrow chin and a long nose. Small brown eye and thick lips. He gave a short laugh at something one of the others said.

They spoke in whispers, too low for me to make out what they said from the sidewalk. I was going to have to get closer to hear their plan.

I could have scared the hell out of them from inside the spell, but I wanted to know what they were thinking. Was this just a series of pranks to them? Had someone sent them to do this to get back at Cameron or was this just mischief of their own making?

I hurried to the driveway where the shell of the haunted house now stood. It was a tall, wooden structure that really did look like a small house built on the two car-wide laneway. The exterior panels had the look of weathered wood, faded and streaked, the boards cracked and old. The front had a small porch and a bay window sticking out. A wooden sign with Woodcrest Haunted House spelled across it in raised letters in a cracked, speckled black hung from the awning that sprouted out about a foot from the front of the house over the porch. On the dark red door hung another sign that read Closed for Reeper-airs.

I hurried up the narrow walk that paralleled the driveway and the front lawn. The iron fencing still closed the lawn off from here until it stopped just before the side stairs leading to the porch. I reached the open part of the fence and slipped onto the grass.

If I hadn't been covered by the spell, I was sure the crunch of grass under my feet would have attracted attention. As it was, none of the three boys looked up. They stayed huddled in a group in front of Boris.

I stepped closer and closer still until I was just a short pace away. Any closer and I couldn't be sure I could dodge fast enough if one of them moved toward me. If one of them touched me, that would negate the distraction element of the spell. It was designed to keep me out of sight, not out of reach.

"You sure Robbie said that?" one of the boys asked.

The one without the hood up nodded. "He said this guy Rogers is dope. He'll pay anything to get one'a these things back."

"I don't know, man," said the third boy. His voice was high and had a slight squeak at the end like his voice hadn't quite broken yet. "Mr. Rogers' been real good to our school."

"You want inta the Cresters or not?" snapped the bareheaded boy.

"Easy, blue, he's just talkin'," said the second boy.

"And I'm just tellin'," said Blue. "We doin' this or not."

I was never going to get a better set up line.

"How about not?" I said loudly.

I took several steps back to avoid the swinging arms of the second boy as he spun around. All three were looking wildly around, eyes wide and faces pale in the yellow light.

"What the fuck was that?" squeaked the third boy.

"Nothin'," said Blue. "Wasn't nothin.'"

Time to up my game.

I ducked around the second boy and came up behind Boris. I grabbed onto both arms and turned to the left. I remembered Cameron had mentioned that Boris had originally been designed for movement, but as he had other moving props, he just kept Boris as a static one.

But tonight, Boris was static no more.

I heard the click and grinding of a gear. Boris jerked to the left, then jerked again as I applied more pressure.

Under my coat, I could feel myself starting to sweat from the effort and all I'd gotten was a bare inch of movement. There had to be a better way.

The cane, handle tucked into the pocket of my coat, tingled.

That was an idea.

I released Boris and grabbed the cane.

I could feel magic vibrating off it. I imagined I could use it as a controller, like something you would use on a battery-powered car.

Only my car would be Boris.

I touched the cane to Boris's shoulder.

The tingling in my hand increased. I pulled the cane back then jerked it to the right.

Boris jerked too.

I tilted the head of the cane forward.

Boris reached forward, and then forward again as I tilted the cane more. And then more.

Until one of Boris's static hands touched the shoulder of Blue.

The boy screamed.

The other two boys screamed as well, the third one's voice rising to a squeak before cracking.

I yanked the cane around, causing Boris to jerk to the left, as if he was tracking the screams.

Seeing Boris move made the boys loose all sense.

They scrambled backward, their feet slipping on the grass. Their bodies leaned too far back and they fell on their rumps. The third boy lay gasping and sobbing on the ground but the second boy and Blue both fumbled around, trying to get to their feet. The second boy clawed up hunks of grass from the lawn, trying to get enough purchase to push himself up. Blue managed to get to his knees.

Time for a little more from Boris.

I shoved the bottom of the cane forward and to the left.

Boris's left leg lifted and slammed down. With a shove of the cane to the right, Boris's other leg lurched forward as well.

The second boy threw the handfuls of grass at Boris, mewling high up in the back of this throat. Blue fell forward onto his face and started trying scramble/crawl away while flat on his stomach.

That probably did it.

I touched the cane to Boris's shoulder again and felt the magic drain away, leaving Boris inert. Then before I could reveal myself, I heard a loud click.

"Nobody move," Mallory said. He stood on the other side of the fence with his gun out. The boys froze.

"Noel, you in there?" Mallory called.

I stepped behind Boris then tapped the cane on the ground. A quick recitation and I broke the spell. I poked my head out from behind the static zombie.

"Right here," I said. "Our vandals were going to steal this prop and ransom it back to Cameron Rogers. Part of some kind of initiation, am I right, boys?"

The second boy and Blue stared at me in astonishment, mouths opens, eyes wide. The third boy still lay back in the grass, totally defeated.

"That's a criminal offense," Mallory said. "Could be serious jail time. On your feet, boys. Hands on the fence and feet apart. Let's move!"

The whip-snap tone in Mallory's voice broke the boys frozen stance. They scrambled to their feet, shoving at each other in order to obey Mallory's instructions first.

As the boys settled into a line along the fence, Mallory called for backup. Within half an hour, a cruiser had arrived to pick up the boys. All three were handcuffed and piled into the back seat of the cruiser. Just before one of the officers closed the door, I heard the second boy say, "I swear that zombie moved on his own. There weren't nobody behind him."

The door clicked shut before either of the boys or the officer could reply.

As the cruiser pulled away, Mallory turned to me, one eyebrow raised.

"You forgot to wake me," he said. "Sounds like I missed the zombie attack."

"You know how kids have overactive imaginations," I said.

Mallory stared at me and then shook his head. "You sure you aren't secretly the son of whoever looks after Halloween?"

CHAPTER

FIVE

At seven in the morning, the cemetery in Cameron Rogers's front lawn was back to looking more normal which, as I walked up the stone steps to his porch, struck me as an odd thing for me to think.

Maybe I had been hanging around this haunted house display for too long.

When I rang the doorbell, Cameron's wife Suzanne answered. A tall, willowy woman with black hair that spilled like a curtain over her shoulders, she wore a long sleeved dress of burnt umber that fell to her knees. She greeted me with a welcoming smile.

"Hello Mr. Kringle," she said. "You look like you could use a cup of coffee."

"I wouldn't say no," I said.

She laughed. "Come in. Cam is just finishing up with Stacy."

I followed her into the house.

Unlike the gothic look of the cemetery outside, the interior of the house was decidedly modern, with a large airy entrance way and an open concept living room that expanded into the kitchen.

A tasteful, dark blue living room set of an L-shaped couch and two matching chairs created a cozy space inside the massive room. To the side, floor to ceiling book cases managed to give the impression of a separate library space, complete with two additional high-backed, arm chairs, these in dark brown to match the shelves.

Past the kitchen, I spotted an open door that appeared to lead into a dining room with a long wood table and matching chairs tucked in on the sides.

Suzanne's black heels tapped on the marble floor as she crossed behind the kitchen island that separated it from the living room. She grabbed another white mug and set it down beside the two that sat on the island.

The gurgle of a coffee maker finished, sending the warm aroma of coffee wafting through the air. I inhaled it as if the aroma itself could give me back the hours of sleep I'd missed the night before. Mallory had insisted I stay the entire time he was booking the boys. I'd barely had the chance to *wink* back to my apartment for a change of clothes before heading here.

Suzanne poured coffee into all three mugs before sliding one over to me.

"We have actual cream and sugar if you like," she said.

"Right now, black is perfect," I said.

I took a sip. The hot brew scalded my tongue but the sharp flavour exploded in my mouth. I could feel myself waking up more with just one mouthful.

"I hope it's not too strong," she said. "Cam likes it extra strong as he's only allowed one cup per day. He likes to make it the equivalent of two or three cups if he can."

Even as I swallowed my first mouthful, I could feel the caffeine starting to hum through my system.

"This is perfect," I said. "I need a good jolt today."

"I hear you captured the culprits."

Cameron's voice bellowed from the front foyer. A moment later he stepped into the living room, kitchen area. He wore dark grey pants with a crisp white shirt. A stylish pale yellow tie was tied around his neck, held with a silver clip.

He crossed behind the kitchen island to reach his wife. He leaned over to kiss her cheek.

"How's Stacy doing?" she asked.

"Not bad. I think she needs another pass on it tonight but she should be good for her history test on Wednesday," he said.

"That's good to hear," she said. "I'll leave you both to it." She slid over a cup of coffee to Cameron before she picked up her mug and slipped away behind him. Her shoes tapped on the hard wood floor as she crossed to the stairs and headed up.

"She's not so big on Halloween," he said. "She likes it well enough, but not as much as I do. As long as I keep collecting money for charity, I can keep doing it as far as she's concerned."

He took a sip of coffee. I mimicked him. The temperature had lessened, making it easier to drink and the richness easier to taste.

"Ah, nectar of the gods," Cameron said. "So it was kids?"

"It appears so," I said and set my mug down on the dark grey marble countertop. "I apprehended three of them planning to steal Boris the zombie to ransom back to you. It sounded like it was a gang initiation."

Cameron shook his head. "Unbelievable. They must have been from well outside the neighbourhood. Everyone here knows I raise money for the hospital. I can't believe anyone around here would do this."

"Well, you tell me if you recognize them." I pulled out a sheet of paper and unfolded it. Mallory had printed a copy of each mug shot photo without the identifying numbers onto one sheet of paper. The resolution was a little grainy but each boy's face was visible enough.

I slid the paper across the island to Cameron.

He took another mouthful of coffee before picking up the paper. Then he stopped. His cheeks puffed out on either side of his face like a puffer fish. His eyes widened as he stared at the paper.

"Mr. Rogers, swallow the coffee," I said.

I wasn't sure he heard me but the Adam's apple in his throat moved. His cheeks deflated. His mouth opened.

"I can't believe it," he said. "These boys. I know them."

"They live near here?" I asked.

"Three streets over." He lifted his chin, indicating north. "They've been coming to the haunt every year since they were little. Their parents used to hand them the money so they could pay for themselves."

He looked bewildered at the thought. I felt for him. Here he was, sharing his passion with the neighbourhood, doing good for the community, and teenagers in that community were betraying him.

Maybe there was a way to teach them a lesson and restore Cameron's faith in them.

"The police are holding the boys until their parents pick them up today," I said. "If you want to charge them with trespassing, you can. But maybe instead you can put them to work on your haunted house. Make them see how much work goes into it."

The dismayed look on Cameron's face faded, replaced one of contemplation.

"I could do that," he said. "I could contact their parents and work out a schedule. They could see how much work it is and also how much it gives back."

I nodded. "I don't think you'll have any trouble with them again."

"Thanks so much, Mr. Kringle," he said. "I really appreciate everything you've done. It really takes a load off my mind."

"My pleasure," I said. "But please call me Noel."

"Only if you call me Cam."

"All right, Cam."

"Be sure to send me your invoice and I'll pay it right away. Having peace of mind at this time of year is worth everything."

"I'll do that," I said. "But your retainer pretty much covers it. I'll tell you what. Let's call it even if you let me come to see your haunted house for free."

He laughed. "You bet! You can even come on the friends and family night the week before Halloween. Then you can go through as many times as you like."

"May I bring along my associates?" I asked. "There are only two of them."

"Sure. Why not?" Cameron said.

I drained my mug and set it down on the countertop.

"Please thank your wife for the coffee," I said. "And I'll see you the week before Halloween."

Cameron followed me to the front door where he stopped me to shake my hand. "I'm so grateful for what you've done," he said.

I smiled at him. "I'm glad I could help. I'm sure the rest of the season will be smooth sailing. Or smooth scaring."

Cameron laughed at my terrible joke and waved before closing the door.

I walked down the stairs, glancing at the cemetery

spread out on either side of the walk. Now that I had spent some time here, it didn't seem all that scary. I could appreciate the hard work and craftsmanship that went into making it look so authentic. I still didn't see how it couldn't be finished as it was. I was looking forward to seeing it the week before Halloween.

I was sure all Cameron's problems were well and truly over.

Little did I know.

Despite the huge cup of coffee, I still felt tired after being up most of the night. Instead of heading back to the office, I went home instead.

I made sure I travelled far enough away from Cameron's house to not attract any attention. Then I *winked.*

And landed in my living room.

Morning sunshine shone through the two narrow windows in the living room wall, illuminating the taupe leather sofa that faced them and highlighting the thick, dark chocolate rug under my feet.

I kicked off my shoes, digging my toes into the rug and then shrugged off my navy pea coat. Normally I hung it up one of the coat hooks near the front door but that involved moving farther away from the bed. Instead, I draped it over the back of the sofa and leaned the cane beside it. I dropped my red scarf and hat on the glass coffee and headed for the bedroom.

Past the kitchen that looked onto the living room, then down the hall. The bathroom was on the right and just past that was the bedroom on the left. I didn't bother turning the light on, just took a few steps into the darkened room and flopped onto the queen-size bed. Just before I fell asleep, I sent a magical request to the cane to wake me in an hour.

Then I was out.

I AWOKE TO SOMETHING POKING ME IN THE SIDE.

I pushed it away and tried to go back to sleep, but it started poking again. It wasn't anything sharp, just a round, flat end, but it got more insistent the longer I lay in bed.

Finally I sat up. My brain felt mushy, foggy. I must still be dreaming because I saw a cane floating beside my bed.

There was a cane floating in the air beside my bed.

Oh right. I'd told it to wake me in an hour.

"Good job," I said and grabbed it as I slid off the bed.

In the bathroom, I splashed water on my face. The shock of cold wiped the remaining fog from my mind. I dried my face and then brushed my teeth. As I swirled the minty toothpaste around in my mouth, I contemplated the claw foot bathtub. Did I want to take a shower? A shower curtain hung from a rod that encircled the tub. Mrs. Pealers, my landlady who lived on the main floor of the three storey walk-up, had apologized about the tub but I liked it.

Except when the shower curtain leaked onto the bathroom floor, which happened more often than not.

I didn't really feel like mopping up a wet floor now. Maybe tonight.

I rinsed my mouth and headed for the living room.

It was just after nine, plenty of time to get into the office and get a full day's work done. Or maybe half a day. One hour of sleep wasn't going to make up for a lost night.

I pulled on my coat and hat. Gathered the scarf and the cane, and *winked*.

On the way into the office, I stopped at the nearby coffee shop for a bagel and coffee. With food and more caffeine to fortify me, I could face the mundane work of writing up the invoice for Cameron Rogers.

What I couldn't face was Venir.

I carried my coffee and bagel up the four flights to my office. The stairs were mostly unpainted concrete walls, smelling vaguely stale and antiseptic. The hallway was dimly lit, making the etched engraving on the window of my office door stand out.

SC Investigations. It always gave me a little tingle when I saw it. My company, my job.

I opened the door.

Three women and two men sat in my waiting room. They all looked up as I walked in.

I had never had so many people in my office. Were they all separate clients? Here about a single case?

Why were they so dressed up?

The door to my interior office was closed. I crossed the floor with five pairs of eyes watching me. I wondered if I was going to stumble over my own feet or drop my coffee or something. In the crook of my elbow, the cane quivered against me, reacting to my nervousness.

Settle down.

Good advice to it and me.

I reached my door without falling on my face. I put my bagel on top of the coffee lid and grabbed the door knob.

When I opened the door, Venir was sitting in my chair, across from a young man in a navy blue suit.

"Oh, ah, this is Noel Kringle, president of the company," Venir said.

The young man stood up. "Pleasure to meet you, sir."

He held out his right hand. Mine was full of coffee and bagel. I gave a weak wave with my left hand.

"Yes, nice to meet you," I said. "Would you mind stepping out? I'd like to confer with my associate."

"Of course."

I managed to slide over to the side of my desk, allowing the young man to slip past me and out the door. I set my coffee and bagel down on the desk before I closed the door. I then turned to face Venir where he sat bolt upright in my chair. Instead of his usual t-shirt or flannel shirt and jeans, he wore a white shirt under a grey suit.

He had even combed his mass of white curls and neatened the white beard that decorated his chin.

"What is going on?" I articulated each word very carefully, just to make sure he heard every one.

"You've been so busy," he said. "I thought I'd take care of it, boss."

"Take care of what?"

"See, there's lotsa interest. I've already done a first cut of the resumes."

I leaned over my desk, until my face was barely two inches from his. I could even smell the slight candy cane scent of his aftershave.

"What in the burning coals do you think you are *doing?*"

My voice started in a low hiss and ended almost in a yell.

Venir pressed his lips tight together. Then puffed out a breath.

"I was tryin' to help you, kid," he said.

I dug my nails into the desk blotter. Beside me, the cane quivered, hitting the side of my desk. The sight of it caused a flash of alarm to cross Venir's face.

"Hey, is that…," he started.

"Answer my question," I snapped.

He yanked his gaze back to me. A slightly petulant look started to tighten his features but when I narrowed my eyes, he looked away.

"I was interviewin' for the receptionist job," he mumbled.

I could feel heat rising inside me. My heart beat quickened as my temper flared. But I couldn't yell at him with all of those people in the waiting room.

I took a deep breath and let it out slowly.

"Venir, I told you I am not hiring a receptionist. We do not need a receptionist. I do not have the money to pay for a receptionist. There is no space for a receptionist in this office."

"I found a bigger office," he said. "It's got two extra rooms and a larger waiting area. We could totally add a desk in there..."

"No!" I was sure my yell could be heard in the waiting room. It could probably be heard through the entire building.

"No receptionist. No other office. Just no," I said. I pointed at the door behind me. "You are going to get rid of those people. You are going to tell them you made a mistake. You are going to shut down whatever ad you are running. And you are never going to do anything like this again without my express permission. Do you hear me?"

The Elf gave a curt nod. My brother had never liked Venir. He had warned me that the ex-Christmas Elf was impetuous and couldn't be trusted. But I had never found that to be the case. This was the first time he'd ever done anything like this behind my back.

"Now, Venir," I said.

"Yes, sir."

He climbed off the chair, head down. Through the mass of his white curls, I could see his pointed ears jutting up above his head.

"Make sure to mask your ears," I reminded him. "Those people out there won't understand what they're seeing."

"Right. Sorry."

He managed to slip by me without touching me even though there was less than an inch between me and the wall. Just like my dad who could fit through the smallest of spaces on Christmas Eve.

I waited until he had left, closing the door behind him, then I hung up my coat on the nail on the back of the door. I set my hat on the desk and moved over to my chair. I sat down, listening to the regular squeak of the seat. I rested the cane in the corner by the window.

By now my toasted bagel was cold and my coffee was tepid. I could have warmed them with some magic but didn't bother. I didn't have enough to spare on that kind of triviality.

Normally I would ask Venir but I wasn't going to ask him for anything for a while. He probably wasn't going to be too happy with me but that was fine, I wasn't too thrilled with him either. I understood how he wanted to expand the business and work hard at making it grow. He was an ex-Christmas Elf and they lived to work. I was sure the pace of my work was nowhere near what he was used to.

That didn't excuse him from going against what I'd said.

I had said no. Hadn't I?

I remembered telling him I didn't earn enough for more staff. I remembered saying there wasn't space for a receptionist.

But nothing quite so blatant as a direct 'no.'

I sighed and took a sip of lukewarm coffee. So it was partly my fault. Elves weren't known for being the best at picking up social cues, especially when they got an idea in their head. I should have been more direct with Venir from the first time he mentioned it.

I wouldn't forget again.

I finished my bagel in two bites and washed it down with the tepid coffee. Just as I flipped up my laptop screen, my desk phone rang. I grabbed the receiver.

"SC Investigations. Noel Kringle speaking."

"This home security video you got me lookin' at," Shirl's voice blurted over the phone. "It's more 'n static on it."

"Hello to you too, Shirl," I said.

"Yeah, hey," she said. "So, you comin' by to take a look?"

"What's wrong with it?" I asked. "Will you need more than an hour to decipher it?"

"I worked on it for five hours," she said. "It's still all blocked. You need to come look."

Five hours. I definitely couldn't afford a receptionist or a larger office. I hoped I'd be able to continue to afford this one.

I sighed. "I'll be right over."

She hung up without saying goodbye. Shirl Trombley was never one for niceties.

I gathered my hat, coat and scarf, slipping everything on, then I paused, looking back at the cane.

I should put it back in the bottom drawer of my desk. I had enchanted the drawer when I first got the desk. It could never be opened by a normal person and it was useful for storing magical items inside. I even used it to keep an extra set of clean clothes inside. When I needed to swap out, I could stuff my dirty clothes inside and the drawer would return them to my apartment, drawing forth another set of clean clothes from my closet at home.

It was the perfect holding place for a magical cane. But I kind of liked having it along. I didn't know if it was influencing me to keep it around or if something in the back of my head thought I might need it, but I definitely felt like I should keep out.

Fine. But it wasn't getting out of my sight.

I grabbed it and *winked*.

CHAPTER

SIX

Clouds had returned to the sky, bringing along a chill dampness that threatened afternoon showers. My go-to anchor closest to her apartment was an alley just south of her apartment building on Bathurst. The air hung heavy with exhaust from the never-ending stream of cars along the street as I walked along the cracked sidewalk to her brownstone.

Shirl lived and worked on the top floor at the very end of a narrow hallway with the thinnest carpet I had ever felt under my feet. I considered gifting the entire building an upgrade in hall carpeting for Christmas but Shirl told me the landlord would be too suspicious of its sudden appearance.

Before I even reached her door, Shirl stuck her head out into the hall. Even in the sickly yellow hall lighting, her dark skin shone. She wore jeans and a taupe sweater with the sleeves pulled up to her elbows. As usual, she had her long braids wound up in a large circular tower on top of her head. Its height still didn't help her come up past my shoulder.

She gave me a slight nod as she held her slightly battered metal door open for me. I slipped inside ahead of her.

As usual, the living room was stacked with cardboard boxes that encircled the entire room, leaving just enough space for a large L-shaped desk which contained three large monitors and a wireless keyboard and mouse. A slim desktop sat tucked underneath on the floor.

"Want coffee?" Shirl asked as she slid past me. She paused in the entrance to the living room, one hand pointing toward her kitchen. I shook my head. I could already feel the caffeine from my lukewarm coffee starting to course through my veins. After the large mug at Cameron's house, a third coffee in the morning would leave me bouncing off the walls.

"Did they break the security system?" I asked.

She shook her head. "Pull up a seat."

As she drew back her blue leather chair, she gestured at a bar stool at the end of the desk. A stack of three boxes stood teetering on it.

"Is it okay if I move these?" I asked.

"Sure, just don't drop 'em," she said.

Carefully, I picked up the boxes, thinking they were probably heavy but I was surprised to find they weighted barely anything. I set them on the floor and picked up the stool to carry it around to where she sat.

"Are you sure there's something in those boxes?" I asked. "They were awfully light."

"SSDs," she said. "Several grand worth. Lighter 'n faster than hard disks." She tilted her head at me. "I could put one in that crap laptop o' yours for cost."

Shirl had been bugging me to let her build me a system since I'd met her but I didn't need the kind of high powered systems she built.

"That's okay," I said. "Show me what you've got on the security video?"

"Park it." She sat cross-legged on the chair with the keyboard in her lap. Her fingers flew over the keys.

The monitors flared to life. The middle one showed a shimmer of silver static. The left and right ones showed black screens with white coding on them.

"I tried several different ways of cleaning it up," she said. "Thought they might be usin' some kind of jamming equipment. But it doesn't clear up in the usual way."

She flipped through several screens on the left and the right, showing me her work and discussing the different things she tried. Her voice faded to a comfortable buzz in the background as I focused on the middle screen. The static shimmered and rippled from the left to the right and back again. First it was a snow of white against a black background, then it shifted to silver on black. Then the colour seemed to change. The black became the static and the silver was the background. Then it shifted back again. And back again. On and on. Back and forth.

I could feel myself swaying from side to side. Or maybe it just felt like that inside my brain. It was soothing and comforting. An easy rocking, back and forth.

Back and forth.

Back...and forth.

Back and... forth.

Back...and...forth.

The silver-black static filled my vision. My heart beat echoed in the same rhythmic flow of the ripple movement. I could feel it tingling up my nerve-endings.

The same way magic tingled up my spine.

Wait...what?

I tried to hold onto that thought, but it flowed away, swept off by the swaying rhythm.

Back...and...forth.

The silver-black static filled my mind, crowding out any thought. All I could see were the rippling, flowing waves. There was no other sensation. No sound, no touch, no scent, no taste. Not even the lingering taste of lukewarm coffee.

What was...?

Coffee...

I latched onto that. I remembered the taste of lukewarm coffee in my mouth. A little bitter, but good enough to wash down a cold bagel.

Yes! A cold bagel with warm cream cheese.

I held the taste of it in my mind, shielding it from the ebb and flow of the static that I could feel was trying to rip the thought away from me. But I couldn't let it, couldn't let it take the bagel and coffee the same way it had taken every-thing else.

Including me.

I couldn't remember who I was. Didn't know where I was or if I was. There was only the static, and a glimmer of a memory of coffee and a bagel.

But already I could feel it starting to unravel under the relenting hammering waves of the static.

It was never-ending and I would never be able to stop it or fight it for long. I was going to lose the only memory I had left and then I would be lost for good.

Help, I needed help!

I tried to shout it but I didn't know what shouting was or how to do it. I focused on the thought and tried to send it forth. Tried to sent it out of me.

Tried to cast it off.

Cast it out.

Cast it like a spell.

Help!

A jolt of pain hit me in the side. For a moment, the static wavered, shimmering back to white on black, then it stabilized.

The jolt came again. Then another, and another.

Something was hitting me. Hitting me in the side.

I remembered I had a side.

"What the fuck?" a woman's voice shouted.

I felt my body again, the right side throbbing. Then I heard a screech of metal on wood. Felt myself tipping...

Tipping backward.

I slammed onto the floor, landing on my back. My vision blurred, darkened for a moment, and then came back.

I blinked at the speckled white ceiling that filled my vision. Then I heard a thunk of plastic on wood. The slap of shoes hitting the floor. A woman's face appeared above me.

"What the fuck are you doing?" she asked.

Shirl. It was Shirl. The memory of her flooded back into my mind. A moment later, everything came back. The North Pole. Dad. KJ. Venir. Toronto. Even me.

Noel Kringle.

I had almost been lost.

I felt like I was being pressed down against the floor, held on my back. My mouth tasted as dry and cracked as old plastic lids. I managed to part my lips and wet them with my tongue that felt almost swollen.

"Turn off the static," I whispered.

Shirl leaned closer. The scent of her filled my nostrils, making it easier to breathe. Anchoring me more into the here and now.

"Static," I said. "Turn it off."

A puzzled look settled on her face but she knew better than to ask at the moment. Her face vanished. I didn't hear anything but a pressure I had been feeling above me seemed to lessen.

I could push myself up now if I wanted.

I became aware of my hands and felt them against the floor. It felt cool and smooth. I applied pressure and felt myself move as I pushed. Soon all my muscles were working again.

I sat up.

The stool lay on its side in front of me. Shirl's desk was above me but if I tilted my head back far enough I knew I would be able to see that middle monitor.

Be able to see that static.

The thought filled me with terror. My body cringed. I found myself trembling violently.

"Noel, what is it?"

Shirl knelt beside me. She grabbed my shoulders and turned me to face her.

"Static?" I asked.

"It's off," she said. "Do ya want me to wipe the disk? I can wipe it."

I shook my head. Whatever it was, I didn't think it could affect me if it wasn't playing.

I hoped.

"What happened?" I asked.

"You tell me," she said. "I was tellin' ya 'bout what I did to clear up the recording, then that cane of yours starts goin' crazy, hittin' you on the side. You didn't even flinch. Then it hooked onto the stool and pulled it out from under you."

The cane had heard me. My magical connection to it was strong enough that it had heard me calling for help.

Swirling snow, without it, I never would have come back.

I glanced over. The black cane now rested against the

edge of the desk, no more inanimate than a regular cane. But I could almost feel it tuned toward me. Ready.

"You should get ridda that thing," Shirl said. "What you doin' affecting a cane for? First that hat and now a cane?"

"That cane just saved my life." My voice sounded stronger. The trembling I felt was getting under control.

An aftereffect. Just my body's reaction to shock.

Sure, I could tell myself that. And I would.

Shirl tilted her head. "What are you talkin' about?"

"There's something in the static, something powerful. More powerful than I've ever felt. Magic or a spell of some kind. I was almost lost inside of it."

"Really? I been looking at it on and off for hours. How come it don't affect me?"

"You don't have any magic, Shirl," I said. "You're immune to it. This static was specifically geared to any magical creature."

My stomach clenched. Had it been geared toward me?

The thought terrified me.

Who else would it have been geared toward? I didn't know of any other magical investigator. Had someone or something decided to get rid of me?

I had to figure out what this was and who had done it but that was going to be almost impossible without showing it to someone who was magical. How I could risk another magic user's life just to know?

But how could I not investigate this? If it was ever widely

used it could create pandemonium in the Magical Realms. Not to mention endanger any magic user here in the Human Realm.

Like my entire family.

I was going to have to figure out what it was and who had done it and I was going to have to figure out a way to do that that wouldn't trap me or endanger anyone else.

Easy peasy.

Like trying to separate out the individual snowflakes in a snow storm.

But how could I investigate it when I couldn't even watch it?

"C'mon, up you get," Shirl said. She grabbed hold of my arm and yanked. I managed to stand without feeling like I was going to fall over. The shock effect had almost completely worn off but I could feel myself tense as I turned toward Shirl's desk.

The middle monitor was dark, turned off.

I almost sagged with relief.

Shirl picked up the fallen stool and set it upright. She gave me another look with her head tilted to the side.

"You sure you're all right?"

"Now that it's off, I'm fine," I said. "I don't want you to have that on when anyone magical is in here, not me, Venir, or Palle. No one. In fact, don't play it around anyone else at all. I don't even like the idea of you looking at it."

"It don't affect me," she said.

"Not yet it doesn't," I said, "but maybe it'll learn."

She shook her head. "You crazy. Sit down. Go on, sit."

I sat back down but swiveled on the stool so my back was to the monitor.

Just in case.

Probably paranoid, I knew, but I wasn't taking any chances. It had been way too close a call.

Shirl disappeared into the kitchen then returned a few moments later with a tall tumbler full of a familiar yellowish liquid. Her gran's famous lemonade. Not exactly the time of year for it but I welcomed the tart flavour.

Shirl handed me the glass. "Drink it slow."

But I had already taken a large gulp. The tartness filled my mouth, followed with a blast of heat that shot down my throat to my belly. Vapours of heat tickled the roof of my mouth making me cough. My eyes watered.

"I tol' you to drink it slow," Shirl said. "I added a little shot of somethin'. Calm you down."

I managed to stop coughing to swipe at my eyes. "A shot of what? Gasoline?"

"Just a little somethin' my gran used to make. When she added it to her lemonade she called it her Real Special Lemonade."

"I bet she did," I said. I took a smaller sip. This time the burning was more of a gentle warmth that spread down my throat and then through my body, not the searing blast from before. I felt the tension in my muscles start to dissolve. I set the glass down on the desk.

"You don't want it?" Shirl asked.

"It's a little much for me in the middle of the day," I said. "But thank you. It did take the edge off."

She shrugged and took the glass away into the kitchen. A moment later she returned and curled up in her blue leather seat.

"So somebody cast a spell on that security camera," she said. "Why'd they be doin' that at that place?"

I opened my mouth to respond, then paused. That was a good question. Why had the spell attached itself to the security camera over Cameron Rogers' haunted house? It couldn't possibly be those kids. Even if one of them had potential and they somehow managed to pull together the ingredients and correct instructions for a spell, they would never have been able to create one so powerful and specialized.

So who had? And why Cameron's home?

This wasn't a simple case of vandalism. Maybe it never had been.

Something was going on and I had no idea what.

"Keep working on it," I said. "Take frequent breaks. I want you calling me to check in every couple of hours. Even if you stop working on it and are working on something else."

"What?" she said. "That's crazy."

"As long as that recording is here, I want you to check in with me. Leave a voicemail. I don't want to take any chances with it." I paused, chewing the inside of my mouth. "Maybe you shouldn't even look at it again. Just lock it up."

"I'm fine," she snapped. "It don't bother me like it did

you. You want me to check in? Fine, I'll call ya every coupla hours. But don't you tell me what I can't do."

She crossed her arms over her chest. Her lips pressed tight together in a thin line. The creases in her forehead deepened.

"Just be careful," I said.

After a moment, the tension in her body loosened. The anger drained from her face, leaving uncertainty.

"You really think it's somethin' bad?" she asked.

"I know it is," I said.

She gave a slow nod. "But you're gonna keep lookin' into it, aren't ya?"

I puffed out a breath. "I think I have to. It came from an amateur haunted house that draws thousands of kids at Halloween. What if they're in danger? I have to do something to stop it."

"Yeah, ya do," she said. "Me too."

Anxiety tightened my chest. Whatever had created that spell was way out of my league but I couldn't let it go. Not with Halloween in a few days. If those children were in danger, hell, even Cameron and his family and friends were in danger from it.

I had to keep going for all of them.

I gave a final nod to Shirl as I slid off the stool.

"Call me in two hours," I said as I stopped just inside the door.

"Yeah," she said but she had already turned toward the

blank monitor. From the way her body leaned forward, I knew she was itching to turn it back on and face the static.

I slipped out and shut the door before the monitor flicked on. Through the steel, I thought I caught a slight hiss from it. I hurried away, feeling it almost follow me all the way out of the building.

CHAPTER

SEVEN

It was too early to head to Cameron Rogers's house so I went back to my office. This time when I *winked* in, I landed in my chair, the springs creaking under me. I stood and took off my coat to hang it on the nail on the back of my door then rested the cane in the corner behind it. Just as I finished and was pulling the door back, the hallway door swung open. A large burly man stepped inside.

For a moment his short, cropped brown hair and his wide flat face remained visible, then they shimmered, falling away to reveal the pale green flesh hidden underneath. At nine feet tall, Palle the troll still had to hunch inside my office but he didn't seem to mind. He wore black pants that stretched across his large thighs but only reached halfway down his calves. His feet were bare, revealing thick claws that clicked on the wood floor. A triple X size sleeveless top strained to cover his chest, the seams bulging. A fabric jacket draped over top that, the sleeves coming just below his elbows.

"Good afternoon, Noel." His deep voice rumbled through the office as he glanced around the waiting room. "Have you picked a receptionist yet?"

I sighed. Venir had got to Palle too.

"I'm not hiring a receptionist," I said. "I don't need one and I don't have the money to hire one."

Puzzlement crinkled the troll's brow. "But Venir said..."

I put up a hand. "I don't care what Venir said. He had no authority to say anything about it. We are not having a receptionist. And while I'm on the subject, we're not moving to another office either."

"Oh," Palle said. "Venir had found..." He stopped, tilting his head at me as my lips pressed tight together. "Of course. This office is fine."

He filled the doorway to my inner office. He could almost but not quite fit into the room with my desk.

I didn't want to hash it out anymore, not with the questions and fears swirling in my mind.

"Palle, have you ever heard of a spell that traps a magic user and causes them to lose themselves in it?"

The troll frowned in concentration. With the great tusks protruding out of the sides of his mouth, a frown on him could look terrifying if you didn't know Palle. He tapped one finger on his chin as he thought.

"Such a spell would be dangerous to cast," he said.

"Unless it was focused on a very specific magic user, it could backfire on the caster. Why would you wish to do such a spell?"

"I wouldn't," I said. "It was embedded into the security tape at a home haunt."

I explained the case to Palle. His brow crinkled in puzzlement.

"This is very strange," he said. "Why would someone cast such a spell on a home celebrating such a sacred day?"

"It isn't considered sacred here, Palle," I said. "It's more of a holiday for kids." I told him about the costumes and kids trick or treating around neighbourhoods, then explained about the haunted house.

"They do not understand its significance?" he asked. "They do not believe in the Thinning of the Veil and Communing with the Ancestors?"

"Not exactly," I said. "That's something they would put into a Halloween horror movie."

Palle shook his head. "I will never understand this place."

"Anyway, I have to go back and check on the house, make sure Cameron is all right and nothing else is affected. I think I may want to talk to those kids again too."

"If you wish, I could come with you," Palle said.

I smiled. "I could use all the backup I can get."

I CALLED FIRST TO FIND THAT CAMERON WAS STILL AT WORK BUT Suzanne expected him home by four. This was his final few days of work before taking the next week and a half off for the Halloween haunt and even during this week, he was only working partial days. I could hear the amusement and affection in Suzanne's voice.

"Do you mind if I come by for four?" I asked. "I have some questions for Cameron and for those kids."

"Of course, come on by," Suzanne said. "I'm sure Cam would be happy to have you here when the kids show up to make a big impression on them."

With Palle along I couldn't make anything else.

"See you then," I said and hung up. I nodded to Palle. "Let's go."

After an almost bewildering variety of streetcars, subways, and buses, we managed to get within a fifteen minute walk of Cameron's house. The air had a tinge of coolness to it, crisp with the scent of leaves.

We left the main street and turned into the residential road. Within a few minutes, the roar of traffic faded to a murmur. The sidewalk was only on one side of the road. The houses had a roughly uniform look, most of them two stories with beige siding. The lawns had a blanched, almost yellowish tinge to them, the look of encroaching decay. Autumn was thick here and I imagined how it would look in winter with snow drifting across the asphalt and piling along the side of the street. I could almost feel it in the air, the thickening cold.

And then I could feel it, condensing around me.

Swirling snow, I was calling it to me!

My breath came out like a mist ahead of me. The crispness had intensified. The little bush I passed suddenly curled its leaves with frost.

"Noel? What's going on?" Palle asked.

"Sorry," I said. "It's me. I'm too connected to cold and I'm pulling it around me."

I took a deep breath and let it out. It started as a mist and then trailed to nothing as I focused on releasing the cold. I could feel it clutching at me, like an eager puppy, trying to hang on.

Not yet, it wasn't time for winter yet.

Soon. But for now, let it go.

The last of the cold faded, leaving behind the crisp scent of earth and leaves.

We turned the corner and I spotted Cameron's house a block away. In the fading light, the cemetery on the lawn looked authentic. The tombstones looked like real stone, not the foam board I knew them to be. The creatures stalking the cemetery looked sinister and ghoulish, like they could rush the fence, grabbing for passersby at any moment.

A shiver of delight ran up my spine.

"Why is there a cemetery in front of that house?" Palle asked as we moved toward it.

"That's the Halloween haunt," I said. "It's not real but it's supposed to look real enough to scare people."

Palle frowned and I almost caught a glimpse of his curved tusks through the mask of his human face.

"Why?" he asked.

"It's part of Halloween," I said. "To scare and be scared, but in a safe way. Everyone knows it's not real but it's real enough to suspend disbelief. It's all for fun. Like movies."

"I see," the troll said but I knew he was still struggling with the concept. He didn't quite understand the appeal of make-believe.

We reached Cameron's house and I led the way up the front walk. I spotted the vampire, Karloff, on the left but Boris was still not in his hiding place on the right. If Cameron was having trouble moving the prop, I was sure Palle could do it easily.

Just as I stepped onto the porch, the front door swung open and Cameron stepped out. He'd changed out of his suit and into jeans and a dark blue pullover sweater. He smiled at me.

"Caught your interest, eh?" he said. "That's how it starts, ya know. Hanging around somebody's haunt. Before you know it, you'll start one of your own."

I laughed. "I don't think that's going to happen. I live in an apartment."

"You'll just have to help out at someone else's haunt," he said. He wiggled his eyebrows. "How about mine?"

I smiled. The man was relentless. "I don't think so. I noticed you don't have Boris back in his spot."

"Not yet. I thought I'd get the kids to do it. And here they come."

He nodded toward the right. I turned. Several houses down, three teenagers were moving towards us, shoulders slouched, heads down. As they crossed the street and paced along the fence toward the front walk, Cameron headed down the steps toward them.

I motioned to Palle and we followed.

Cameron stopped at the base of the walk.

The three boys straggled to a stop several feet away. I recognized the boy called Blue at the front, the other two stayed behind as if hiding.

Cameron turned so he was half facing me and half facing the boys. He gestured toward them.

"This is Billy Blufield, Gavin Clifford, and Steve Kowalsky," he said. "I'm sure you boys recognize Mr. Noel Kringle." He tilted his head toward me.

"And this is my associate, Palle Grunbrand," I said.

Billy Blufield glanced up, his jaw tightening. The other boys flinched.

"Seeing how you were so interested in Boris, I thought you should start by putting him back in his proper place," Cameron said.

"And we're here to make sure it's done right," I said.

Now all three of the boys flinched.

Cameron led them back along the fence and around the corner. Palle and I brought up the rear, although I made sure we stayed far back. The three boys bunched up right behind Cameron, with the one called Steve glancing back over his shoulder several times. Stringy black hair fell over his wide forehead not quite obscuring his wide brown eyes.

Obviously he hadn't forgotten my stunt with the prop and I was sure having Palle beside me, tall, hulking, burly, made quite an impression as well.

If he only knew the truth.

At Cameron's direction, the three boys lifted Boris carefully and carried him through the graveyard. At one point, Gavin, who was hunched over holding onto Boris's legs and was waddling with his feet far apart, bumped into one of the tombstones. Cameron made a concerned noise. Gavin flinched, almost dropping the zombie prop's legs.

Palle stepped forward. With one hand, he gripped the legs of the prop, steadying it. The muscles of his arm barely stirred.

Gavin's eyes bulged. His mouth dropped open, the jaw moving but no words coming out.

"Why don't you grab the end to help Palle?" I said.

The boy still stood frozen, his thin face pale as he watched Palle.

"C'mon, Gav, move it," snapped Blue.

That penetrated Gavin's stupor. He hurried forward and grabbed the fabric of the zombie prop's pants near the shredded cuffs. Palle glanced over his shoulder back to me, raising an eyebrow.

Should he let go?

I nodded. This was part of the boys' penance, to help put things to right in the Halloween display.

Palle released the prop and stepped. All three boys sagged with the weight of the prop but then they continued to shuffle forward.

With Cameron's guidance, they managed to avoid any other tombstones. By the time they reached the bush and Boris's original hiding spot, sweat matted the boys' hair to their foreheads. Billy Blufield, who sported a faux mohawk, shook his head to get his flopping hair out of his eyes. He grimaced as they struggled to pull the prop into the narrow space behind the bush. I felt his gaze slide over me and caught the look of resentment.

Might still be trouble with Blue, although if he focused his resentment on me and not Cameron and the Halloween haunt, it might be fine.

Finally the three boys finished getting Boris back into place. Each one pushed out of the space through the bushes. Even in the cool air, they were sweating. Gavin wiped his arm across his forehead. Steve unzipped his hoodie.

Only Billy Blufield refused to do anything to relieve the effect of his efforts.

Stubborn.

I caught a raised eyebrow from Cameron. He stepped forward to stand by the bush.

"So you think you're done?" he asked.

The boys looked uncertainly at each other. Finally Blue spoke up.

"It's back where we found it," he said.

"It is back," Cameron said, "but it's not the way you found it. Take a look at the eyeline. Is it looking at the walkway up to the house? Are the hands reaching through the bushes? To me, he looks like he's staring over there somewhere."

Cameron gestured behind him toward the sidewalk.

"That's not where the scare is. The scare is having Boris looking right at someone who's on the stairs, his hands reaching up for them. That's the scare."

Gavin and Steve looked confused but Blue had tilted his head, as if considering Cameron's words.

"Maybe they should adjust Boris for the scare," I said. "Why doesn't Gavin stand on the stairs and Billy adjust Boris?"

"Great idea," Cameron said. "Actually, Boris can scare all through the climb on the stairs. Gavin and Steve can stand on the bottom and top stair each. Billy, I'll show you how to make the adjustments."

The boys picked their way back through the cemetery and then raced to the stairs. Steve stopped on the bottom stair and Gavin scurried to the top one. Meanwhile, Cameron murmured to Billy as they pressed into the small space with the prop.

After a few moments of adjusting, both Gavin and Steve nodded that Boris looked good to them. From where I stood, I could barely see Boris's upturned face although I could see his fingers poking out through the bushes.

Cameron led Billy back out of the space. Now, instead of the simmering resentment, interest flushed Billy's face.

"Can I see what it looks like?" he asked.

"Sure," Cameron said. "You boys come back in here."

Gavin and Steve hurried back while Billy ran past on the sidewalk. He skidded as the walk turned up toward the house. Then he slowed and strolled along the walk. He moved his head from side to side, catching both Karloff and Boris in his sights as he walked up the stairs.

"See the effect?" Cameron said. "It's a little creepy but not half as creepy as at night, properly lit. You should see it then."

Billy turned toward him. Eagerness lit up his face. "Can we?"

"Well, I don't know," Cameron said. "You did vandalize my haunt and I had to hire Mr. Kringle to stop you. Letting you come by on Halloween might just be asking for trouble."

Cameron tilted his head toward me.

That was my cue.

"Mr. Rogers, maybe they could help out on Halloween, keep the crowds from being unruly and ruining your work and theirs."

Cameron shook his head in a wide, exaggerated motion. "I don't know. Seems like a lot to expect..."

"If the boys promised," I said.

I turned to look at Blue still standing on the stairs. He tried to mask the eagerness in his eyes with a bland expression on his face. He gave an exaggerated shrug.

"What you want us to be promisin'?" he asked.

"You would have to promise to be here," Cameron said. "You would follow directions, keep the crowds in line peacefully, not talk back, not take off..."

A frown sprouted and deepened on Blue's face as Cameron talked.

"Don't sound like a fun Halloween."

"And," Cameron said with exaggerated slowness. "You would spell out the actors inside the haunted house when they need a break."

"Does that mean...," Gavin said.

"Would we get to...," Steve said.

"You'd get to scare people," Cameron said. "But you follow the haunt rules. No touching anyone. You stay in the spot where you're placed; no running around. No talking in between groups." He stopped and chuckled. "Not that there's any time in between groups on Halloween. Deal?"

As I expected, both Gavin and Steve glanced over at Blue for direction. Blue pretended to consider for a moment, causing some anguished leaning and fist clenching from Gavin and Steve. Then he nodded.

"Deal," Blue said.

"Excellent," Cameron said. "That night Mr. Kringle here will supervise you, along with his friend here. You'll do whatever they tell you to do with no complaints. Got it?"

He looked at all three boys. They nodded, although Blue's face tightened when he glanced at me. I inclined my head to him.

No need to create further antagonism between us.

The muscles in his face loosened but he still had a trace of a frown.

That was probably as good as it would get. He didn't seem like the kind of boy who would forgive me scaring him quite so easily. But at least it was something.

"I'd like to ask a question," I said.

Cameron spread his hands, indicating I should go ahead.

"Why did you put the tombstones all in a line?"

I looked at each of the boys, finally settling my gaze on Blue. His frown deepened again but not with malice.

This time, it was with confusion.

"Tombstones?" Steve said. "What you talkin' about?"

Gavin shook his head. "We didn't touch no tombstones."

Cameron looked puzzled. "You didn't move them?"

"Not us," Blue said. "We just moved the zombie."

Cameron faced me. His lips thinned into a line. He didn't have to say a word, I understood his look.

There was another vandal at work.

CHAPTER

EIGHT

Palle and I stayed a little while longer, watching Cameron supervise the boys as they put out more tombstones, adjusted several, and worked on the lighting. By the time the sun finished setting, Cameron signalled the boys to move away from the far left side of cemetery.

"Check this out," he said. He held a remote in his hand. He turned toward the house and pressed it.

A creepy blue glow enveloped the left side of the cemetery, creating deep shadows and highlighting different tombstones. The tall, blond-haired grave digger loomed in the shadows near the back. When I turned my head a little, it looked like he was moving.

The tombstones, that looked almost real in full light, looked completely lifelike in the gloom and eerie blue light.

"What do you think, boys?" Cameron asked. "Look okay?"

The three boys were lined up along the fence. Each had a look of intense concentration on their face, brows crinkled, mouths pursed. Finally Steve gestured at one of the tombstones at the far left.

"That one needs to be moved a bit. It's too straight."

"Go fix it," Cameron said. "Gavin and Billy, let him know how it looks."

Steve hurried around the fence and climbed inside. He made his way through the graveyard to the stone he had been looking at. Gingerly, he shifted it a little to the left. Gavin and Billy called out instructions.

Cameron watched with a slight smile on his face.

I gave a quiet cough, catching his attention. When he glanced over, I tilted my head to the right. I stepped away, moving along the outside of the fence toward the corner.

Cameron followed.

When we were far enough away that I was sure the boys couldn't hear, I turned to Cameron.

"It sounds like you have someone else vandalizing your display," I said.

"Maybe," he said.

"Maybe?"

"It could just be that they don't want to admit they did it," he said.

"You seemed to think otherwise a little while ago."

A shadow of a frown crossed his face. "I don't like

thinking that someone else has something against my display. Everyone in the neighbourhood knows I collect money for the Children's Healing Hospital. Some kids goofing around I can get." He gestured toward the boys. "But somebody else too? It's too much."

His shoulders sagged. A weariness seemed to settle on his face. I tried to imagine the energy it took to build and look after this display for weeks and then deal with the huge crowds on Halloween.

Almost the kind of energy it took to build and deliver toys around the world all in one night.

"I'll keep an eye on it for the next few nights," I said. "Just to make sure everything is all right."

Cameron shook his head. "I can't..."

I held up a hand to stop him. "On me."

"I can't let you do that," he said.

"Sure you can," I said. "Palle and I can split the duty. It's not a problem at all."

Cameron straightened, standing a little taller. His shoulders shifted back. He smiled.

"Thanks, Noel."

"One of us will be back around ten," I said. "Maybe have some coffee for us in the morning."

"Will do."

He shook my hand and turned back to the boys. They were busy adjusting the tombstone by inches, arguing about which way looked better.

I nodded to Palle and we retreated back into the shadows. When we were far enough away and I was sure no one else was watching, I gave Palle a signal and we *winked.*

My desk lamp was shining on the desk blotter when I landed in my chair. Palle's large form filled the space outside my door as he landed in the waiting room. A sharp hrmph cut through the air.

I glanced across my desk.

Venir sat in one of the hard-backed chairs across from me. An unlit cigar was tucked into the side of his mouth, deepening the frown he wore. His arms were crossed over his chest. The slick white shirt and grey dress pants had been replaced with red flannel shirt over worn blue jeans.

"Something on your mind, Venir?" I asked.

"You workin' a case?" he asked. "Without me?"

"It would be with you if you hadn't had to spend your time getting rid of all of those applicants."

His lips thinned. His glare was full of rebellious anger. My heart beat quickened in response. I could feel my own temper rise.

I did not want a shouting match in the middle of my office.

I took a deep breath and let it out slowly.

"What do you know about Halloween?" I said.

My question had the desired effect. Confusion crossed the Elf's face. His lips dipped into a frown, the cigar sagging in the corner of his mouth. The pointed tips of his ears quivered through the white curls on top of his head.

"Halloween?"

"It's the case we're working on," I said. "A home haunt display is being vandalized. We've caught a group of boys who did part of it but some other vandal is at work."

"But isn't Halloween evil?" Venir asked.

"It's a holiday like any other," I said. "Our client raises money for the Children's Healing Hospital. Thousands per year as a matter of fact."

Venir's eyes widened. "Really?"

"Really. He also entertains thousands of children who come through his pretend haunted house." I let a trace of a smile show on my lips. "Almost like someone else we know."

Venir sucked in a sharp intake of breath.

"Yer dad don't scare kids..."

"No, but he entertains them," I said. "Being scared in an environment you know is safe is fun too."

The Elf's shaggy brows furled on his forehead. "I guess."

"But someone is threatening that, and I don't mean the boys. There's something magical at work."

Venir leaned forward, gesturing with his unlit cigar. "See? That Halloween stuff ain't no good."

I felt my anger bubbling under the surface again.

"Does that mean you're aren't interested in working this case?"

In the waiting room, the floor creaked as Palle shifted so he could press closer in to the doorway. A frown bowed his tusks downward.

Venir jerked upright. "I didn't...I didn't say that," he sputtered.

"Good," I said. "Then I don't want to hear anything more about your opinions on Halloween, especially in front of the client."

The Elf nodded, his head bobbing up and down. "Yeah, sure, 'course."

My anger drained away, draining my energy at the same time. I leaned back in my chair to stop from sagging. The abundance of coffee and the nap didn't replace a full night's sleep and I was still feeling the effects.

Maybe it wasn't just Venir's eagerness to expand the company that was keeping my temper short.

I nodded and smiled at him.

"Good," I said. "Palle is going to watch over the display tonight. I want you to investigate something that would affect a home security system."

I described the DVD display that Shirl was working with and the effect it had on me.

"I don't want you going near it," I said. "But we need to know what could cause that or who could cause it."

"I can't really tell unless I see it myself," Venir said.

I shook my head. "It's too dangerous. I don't want you risking it. Just see if you can find out what kind of spell would have that effect and who or what could cast it."

Venir's shoulders sagged but he nodded. "Okay, boss. I'll report back later."

I opened my mouth to respond but he *winked*, disappearing in a moment. I glanced over at Palle who still filled the doorway.

"He wouldn't try to look at that recording, would he?" I asked.

Palle tilted his head at me but didn't say a word.

Damn the halls.

I grabbed the phone and dialed Shirl's number.

It rang once. Twice. Three times.

Maybe she wasn't even home. As far as I knew, Venir couldn't even turn on a computer. Most technology seemed to baffle him.

If Shirl wasn't home, he wouldn't be able to watch the DVD and be affected by it. He would be safe.

Another ring.

Then the phone was knocked off the hook. I heard a voice cursing as if from a distance then it got louder.

"What? Who?"

Shirl's voice, breathless in the phone.

"Shirl, it's Noel."

"He just popped in here." Her tone rise higher in panic. "No warning. I couldn't turn it off fast enough…"

Swirling snow!

"Turn it off," I said. I found myself on my feet, shouting into the phone. "Turn it off now!"

"It's off," she said. "But he's not wakin' up. Noel, he's not wakin' up."

Her voice broke. My heart thudded.

"I'm coming," I said.

I dropped the receiver onto the phone. Through the door-way, Palle's face was twisted with anguish.

"Venir?" he asked.

"Shirl's place. Now."

I *WINKED*, LANDING RIGHT IN THE ENTRANCE TO THE ALLEY, IN FULL view of the street but I didn't care. It didn't matter who saw me.

I had to get to Venir.

Maybe if we were fast enough we could pull him out of it, like the cane had pulled me.

I ran to her door. The buzzer was already ringing. I yanked the door open and was through, Palle at my back.

When we reached her floor, Shirl was standing in the hall.

Several of her braids had come loose from the swirl of hair atop her head. They hung down like limp rope.

Her face was ashen.

She held out her hands as if beseeching me.

My shoes pounded on the thin carpeting as I ran down

the hall. My heart pounded in my chest. My mouth tasted of ashes.

"He still won't wake up," Shirl said as I reached her. Her voice broke in anguish.

I moved past her, through the door. The thud of Palle's steps echoed my own.

Lights blazed in the living room, brighter than I'd ever seen, highlighting all the boxes along the walls. In the centre of the room sat Shirl's desk and computer set up. All three of her monitors were dark.

A small form lay face up on the floor by the edge of the desk. If his eyes had been closed, he would have looked asleep, but the somewhat tense form and staring eyes belayed that.

Venir.

"We have to draw him back," I said. "The cane pulled me out of it. We can do the same for Venir."

"You know how?" Palle asked.

"Just focus on your magic and reach for him," I said.

That sounded like it should work.

Lying on the floor on his back, Venir looked so much smaller, so much more vulnerable. His unlit cigar dangled from his left hand. The white curls seemed faded and limp. The colour of his face was waxy.

I reached out to touch his hand and felt a repelling energy radiating from him. It started about four inches away from his skin and as I brought my fingers closer, the prickling feeling intensified, turning from prickling to jabbing.

Then as my fingers brushed the back of the Elf's hand, it burned.

I yanked my hand away.

On Venir's other side, I could the strain in Palle's face as he reached for Venir's other hand. His tusks dipped down as he frowned in concentration. Sweat beaded on the smooth, pale green skin of his head.

He didn't even touch Venir before he sat back, shaking his head.

"I cannot," he said. "I am sorry, Noel."

It was up to me then.

I took a deep breath and tried again. No, not tried. I would do it this time. I would grab hold of Venir and pull him out of the magical coma or trance or whatever it was that had trapped him.

I had to be at least as powerful as that cane.

My mouth felt dry as I reached for the Elf's hand again. I'd been slow the first time. This time I would just grab it.

Fast.

I grabbed.

Burning flared up my hand, my forearm. I gasped at the shock of it. Around me, the room seemed to flicker, become less distinct. The dark wood of Shirl's computer desk looked dull and faded. The edges of the boxes around the perimeter smeared together into a brownish blur.

Whatever was affecting Venir was trying to pull me down.

Not gonna happen. I was going to pull Venir out.

I leaned back on my heels and strained to pull Venir upward. At least I thought I did. My body felt disconnected. Even though I commanded it to lean back, it hadn't moved.

I hadn't moved.

Blast the halls!

The burning pain in my hand had faded to a dull ache, throbbing in time with my heart beat. But even it seemed less distinct than before.

I was getting trapped too, just not as far down as Venir.

So maybe there was still a way to get out, to get both of us out.

I strained to lift my head toward Palle. I could see the troll just out of the corner of my eye on the right. He looked frozen, head down, looking at Venir.

Was he frozen or was I locked out of his reality?

I had to find a way to reach him.

I took a deep breath and held it in. After a moment, I felt my heart rate begin to slow, then speed up. I puffed the breath out and tightened my grip at the same time.

Burning pain flared up. My nerves seared. I yanked my head up.

And felt it move.

In slow motion, Palle's head lifted, his face turning toward me. A frown of concentration crinkled his face. The tusks at the corners of his mouth dipped down. His brows protruded and pulled together, creasing a line that bisected his forehead. The tips of his pointed ears quivered over top of his bald head.

I focused on his light grey eyes, projecting a command to him.

Help!

The concentrated frown remained. Then his face began to relax. The lines along his forehead smoothed out as his brow relaxed. His tusks lifted as he stopped frowning. I could see a gleam of awareness in his eyes.

He'd heard me, felt me.

Hadn't he?

It seemed impossible to tell. The slow motion movement made it difficult to know.

Focus. I gathered the remnants of my magic together, remembering my mother's special way of weaving her magic into every movement she made. I couldn't move right now, but I could picture those movements in my mind. Over and over, the sweep of my left hand, making the symbol for strength and control. Over and over.

Over and over.

Focusing.

Aiming.

Gathering it together. Projecting toward Palle.

Help me!

This time I definitely saw the troll move. His head jerked upright. Eyes wide. His lips slightly open, as if he was speaking. In the slow movement of his mouth I thought I saw him sound out my name.

His hand shot out and grabbed my forearm.

A cold as deep as pressing bare skin to solid ice burned

through me. A different burn than that scorching my hand. I hissed at the feeling.

But it was working. I could feel it working.

Palle leaned away, tugging on my arm. His movements no longer seemed stuck in slow motion. He grimaced as he pulled and I realized he was probably feeling the effects of whatever was holding Venir down.

Maybe between the two of us we could pull the Elf out.

I looked down at the Elf lying before me. Venir was still unmoving, so still I couldn't even tell if he was breathing. Did he even feel me holding onto his arm? When I had grasped onto the cane I could feel it pulling me upward but there was no sign of awareness in Venir, no response. Even in my mind, I could feel no echo of him, no tingle of his magic on my skin.

Just the burning in my palm from holding on, the powerful suction of the void trying to drag me down.

It was strong enough to pull Palle down too. Then who would be left to help us? Who would be left to figure out what had happened and why?

I had to let go.

I felt myself sagging as my heart clenched. A hollowness made my stomach drop. How could I let go of Venir? How could I abandon him?

No, I couldn't think of it that way. I wasn't abandoning him. I was going to find a way to help him. I couldn't do that if I let myself and Palle get sucked down into the void with him. I didn't have to power or ability to draw the Elf out now but I would find a way. I would never stop looking for a way.

I sucked in a breath. My lungs felt squeezed and constricted, barely letting me get any air. I puffed it out.

And let go.

Palle yanked me back. I fell to the floor, smacking my elbow on the wood. My head bounced off a box behind me. The light dimmed, shimmering before me, then returned as I felt other hands grab my arm.

"Noel, are you all right?" Shirl asked.

I blinked, focusing on her. The tower of her braids looked a little lopsided on her head. Several of the braids hung down, the tips brushing my arm. Her brows drew together in concern.

"I'm okay," I said.

She tugged, helping me to stand. My body moved sluggishly. I felt uncoordinated and staggered as I gained my feet. Shirl steadied me. Palle still sat on the floor beside Venir, gazing down at the Elf.

"Palle, are you okay?" I asked.

The troll nodded. "I am all right, Noel."

"So what 'bout Venir?" Shirl asked. "Is he gonna wake up now?"

I shook my head.

"So you scared the hell outta me for no reason?" she snarled.

"I thought I could pull him out," I said. "The same way the cane pulled me out."

She shook her head, sending the braids whipping around her shoulders.

"Why dinnt you use the cane then?"

It was connected to me. I didn't see how it would work for Venir but it was certainly worth a try.

I took a deep breath, feeling my lungs expand properly again. The constriction of the void was gone. The draining fatigue was falling away. I centred myself and called to the cane. I could picture it where I had left it, leaning in the corner behind the door of my office.

Another deep breath and I put out my hand. Reaching.

A shaft of cool wood nestled in my palm.

The cane had come to me.

I closed my hand around it. Already I felt stronger, more powerful. The cane was used to being used as a conduit. Even here in the Human Realm it seemed to draw a lot of power. It could do a lot of damage if it wasn't contained properly.

But maybe, just maybe, it could also be useful in other ways.

Like pulling Venir out of the void.

Another deep breath and I centred myself, focusing on Venir. I moved the cane toward him, toward his right hand resting at his side. Even as I moved the cane closer, I could feel it pulsating in my hand, its energy reacting to the spell that held Venir.

Any second now, he would feel it too. Any second now, he would reach for the cane. He would grab hold and it would pull him out. He would break free from the spell, be pulled out of the void.

Any second now...

I touched the back of his hand with the cane. Felt the yawning pull of the void, but the cane held it at bay. Protected me.

Venir didn't move.

He didn't react to the touch of the cane. He didn't grab hold of it.

Nothing.

I pressed the cane harder against his hand.

Nothing. Still nothing.

"Noel." Palle's voice sounded distant. As if he was calling me from far away rather than just a few feet. Around him, the room looked faded, indistinct, like an old photograph where the colours had bled out.

I jostled Venir's hand with the cane. Maybe he was just a little deeper down than I had been. Maybe he just needed a little more time.

Even with the cane, I could feel the void pulling at me. Trying to draw me down.

Venir...

Nothing.

Still nothing.

"Noel!" Palle's shout sounded only a little louder. I turned my head. He was right in front of me.

I pulled the cane away.

The room snapped back into focus. Colours flooded in,

sharpening the view. The deep blue of Shirl's chair. The distinct shades of tan of the boxes piled high. The pale green of Palle's skin.

"I did not want you to get lost," Palle said. "I am sorry if I interrupted the spell."

"You didn't," I said. "The cane didn't work. Venir didn't respond to it."

"So what now?" Shirl asked. "How you gonna get him back?"

She looked at me, as if I knew the answer. I glanced at Palle. He had the same expectant expression on his face.

Looking at me. Waiting for me to tell them what we would do next.

Like I would know.

I looked down at Venir, lying still and pale on the hard wood floor.

Swirling snow, what was I going to do?

CHAPTER

NINE

I couldn't leave Venir lying on the floor of Shirl's apartment. Using the cane, I enchanted Palle with a protection spell, allowing him to pick up Venir without being pulled down into the void. Still even as the troll cradled the ex-Christmas Elf in his arms, I could see the strain on Palle's face. He tried to hide it but the thinning of his lips and the deepening of the crease between his eye brows betrayed him.

"I wanna know he's all right," Shirl said.

I gave her a nod as I lifted the cane.

Palle and I *winked.*

We landed in my office.

Palle placed Venir onto the over-stuffed brown sofa in the waiting room. The Elf didn't even take up half the length,

111

looking small and forlorn in his stillness. He was so motion-less I couldn't even tell if he was alive.

"Is he breathing?" I asked.

"I felt a slight rise of his chest when I held him," Palle said. "What do we do now?"

Good question. I wish I had an answer. I glanced back through the door into my office. The window behind my desk showed the darkened sky. It was just after seven but it looked like midnight out there. A sliver of moon hung in the liquid blackness, reminding me of the void. I hoped somehow Venir had some light to cling to while I thought of some other way to reach him.

But having Palle hovering over my shoulder wasn't going to help, especially since we still had a job to do.

I turned back to the troll.

"I'll keep working on it," I said. "Meanwhile you need to go to Cameron Rogers' house for the stake out."

Palle lifted his head, straightening his body as much as he could before his head brushed the ceiling.

"You expect me to leave Venir?" he asked.

"I expect you to do your job," I said. I spread my hands. "Palle, I know how you feel but staying here isn't going to help Venir. Besides, the security system came from Cameron's house so whatever cast that spell that's ensnared Venir has something to do with that house. Not only will you be watching for any further problems with the display, I want you to watch for any sign of magical disturbance.

There's something more going on here. I want to stop it before it affects anyone else."

The tension that had tightened the troll's muscles and made him frown, revealing even more of the gleaming tusks at the sides of his mouth faded. He hunched down again and gave a slight nod.

"I understand. You will contact me if there is any change?"

"Immediately," I said. I stepped forward and put my hand on his forearm. "Be careful, Palle. If you sense anything, do not engage. This is magic that's stronger and more sophisticated than anything I've ever seen. I don't want to lose you in it as well."

A slight smile tugged at the corners of the troll's mouth. "I will be careful, Noel."

I stepped back and the troll *winked.*

Leaving me alone with the unconscious Elf.

I turned back to look at Venir, lying still on the couch. His head tucked down, giving him a double chin look. His curling white hair had a dull, yellowish cast to it. Could it be from the overhead light? It had never caused that dull look before.

Even the colour of Venir's skin looked pale and dull against the red flannel of his shirt. Like he was fading away.

Somehow I had to think of a way to stop this.

But how?

Normally when things got complicated like this, I would

call on Venir to bounce ideas off of but that wouldn't really help here. Would it?

"Venir, can you hear me?" I asked.

Nothing. No response. Not even a hint of energy from him.

"I know you're deep in there," I said, "but I'm going to find a way to get you out. No matter what it takes. Just hang on. Remember who you are. Don't let the void steal every part of you. Keep hanging on."

I stared at him, noticing the slight rise and fall of his chest as he breathed. But there was nothing else, no slight twitch of a finger, no wiggle of a foot. Not even a smidge of a frown.

I had to think of something else. The cane hadn't worked. Maybe I had some other magical talisman that might work. The cane was from the magical realm, derived from the staff of a renegade Fae. I had been the one to shift the staff into a cane. Perhaps that was why I responded to it because it was bound more tightly to me.

What did I have that might be bound to Venir?

I hurried into my office.

And became acutely aware that it was *my* office.

Although Venir worked with me, he didn't have his own space. He didn't really need it as evidenced by how often he took over my seat. But maybe he wouldn't do that if he had his own desk.

I shook my head. I couldn't deal with that right now. Stay focused. Was there anything here that might reach Venir?

I scanned the objects on my desk and felt my gaze drawn to the presents my mother had given me when I'd first opened my office.

The stapler, paper clip holder, silver letter opener, and my leather notebook that magically transcribed my scrawls onto the laptop that sat at the side of my desk. Each of those objects were imbued with some Christmas magic. In the past, they had reacted to other magical objects. Maybe one of them could call to Venir.

I started to reach for the stapler, but stopped as my fingers brushed the smooth black surface.

These weren't the only presents I had from the North Pole.

Dad had given me a magnifying glass.

If there was anything that might connect to Venir, it would be that magnifying glass.

As soon as I picked it up I could feel a residual tingle of magic that lifted my spirits. This just might be the thing that pulled Venir back or at least stopped him from sinking deeper which would allow me more time to find a way to get him out.

I returned to the sofa where the Elf lay. It was going to be a little tricky to put the magnifying glass in his hand without touching him. Any contact might pull me down.

Maybe the cane.

I grabbed it in my other hand then using a couple of fingers of my right hand, I reached for Venir. As soon as I brushed his skin I felt the pull of the void, like a powerful suction. But the cane anchored me to the room even as my perception dimmed.

I had to be fast.

I lifted Venir's left hand and managed to slide the magnifying glass underneath. Then I lowered his hand. His palm touched the handle. For a moment, it rested down then his fingers curled around so he was grasping it.

He'd felt the magnifying glass! Somehow the Christmas magic within had reached him.

"Venir," I said. "It's Noel. If you can hear me, I'm coming to get you. Just hang on. I'll get you out. Hang on."

No response. I didn't expect any.

Then I noticed how tightly his left hand gripped the handle of the magnifying glass.

Had he heard me? I hoped so. I hoped the magnifying glass was anchoring him somehow.

Now I had to figure out a way to get him out.

I stepped away from the couch, leaning on the cane. Fatigue dragged at me. Fighting against the void twice in close succession was exhausting. My thoughts felt sluggish. I had to wake up.

I stumbled across the waiting room to the small bathroom. When I hit the switch, yellowish light flooded the room. The toilet on the right with the sink on the left. Across from the door was the towel wrack, hung with Christmas towels.

Leaning the cane on the sink, I turned on the cold water

tap and let it fill my hands. Then I leaned over and splashed the water onto my face.

The shock of cold made me hiss. My skin tightened. Blood warmed my face. I splashed again and felt the last of the lingering dullness fall away.

I looked into the mirror, dripping water from my bearded chin. Dark circles looked like smudges under my eyes. I groped for the towel and pressed the softness to my skin.

I was stalling and I knew it. Hoping for an idea to pop into my head about how to save Venir.

But nothing came as I folded the white towel and hung it back up. The embroidered Christmas tree hung a little off centre so I straightened it, making sure the red fringe was untangled as well.

Better.

Still no ideas.

I turned off the bathroom light and faced the sofa across the room.

From a distance, Venir looked so small and helpless.

There had to be a way to reach him. I needed help from someone who had more magic than I did. Even Palle didn't have enough.

But I knew someone else who did.

Someone who was going to be really annoyed.

I took a deep breath.

Time to make a call.

I could use the phone, go through the operator, but that

wouldn't convey the urgency I felt. I was going to have to go for direct connection.

And he was gonna be mad.

I took another deep breath and closed my eyes, focusing. I tightened my grip on the cane, feeling the smooth handle against my palm, the tingle of its magic across my skin.

I gathered my magic close around me, then flung it outward, focusing north. All the way north.

To the North Pole.

And called.

KJ help. I need you.

I could feel the echo of my call reverberate through me. Then the smell of cinnamon and ginger snaps filled my nose.

"Noel, what's wrong?"

I opened my eyes.

My older brother KJ, short for Kris Junior, stood just inside the waiting room door. His red flannel shirt was unbuttoned at the collar and had the sleeves rolled up to the elbows. His white hair was slicked back from his head, highlighting his furled brow and his angled cheekbones that he'd inherited from our mother. His white beard, normally trimmed, was now starting to look bushy. It would continue to get bushier and bushier the closer we got to Christmas. Just like his torso would thickened, forcing him to change out of those black leather pants.

"I'm sorry I had to call you, KJ," I said. "But I need help. Venir is caught in a spell and I can't get him out."

The furl deepened as KJ frowned. "Venir? Is he why you

called me? He got himself into a mess and you thought I'd help?"

KJ's voice dripped with disdain. He'd never had much use for the ex-Christmas Elf. In KJ's mind, abandoning a job at the North Pole was abandoning a sacred trust.

Something he'd never quite forgiven me for either.

"He didn't get into a mess," I said. "It's part of a case."

I explained everything. The Halloween display, the kids causing mischief, and the security system. As I talked, the line between KJ's brow deepened. His frown thinned to a straight line.

"So he was careless," my brother said.

"Not careless," I said. "He just happened to *wink* into Shirl's apartment and see the output on the screen."

"Careless," KJ said. "If he had been thinking he would have appeared in the hallway and knocked on her door, given her time to turn her machine off." He shook his head. "He was always like that at the North Pole too. Always getting in the way."

"You mean always going the extra mile," I said. "Always working harder."

My brother glared at me.

I took a breath and let it out. Letting the tension drain from my body. Even when I thought my brother might be gaining some respect for what I did he would find another issue to pick at, another thing wrong.

I wasn't going to let it be Venir. Not this time.

"Look, I just need help getting Venir out of the spell," I said. "Please help me."

The terse expression on my brother's face didn't change as he stalked farther into the room. He glanced at Venir's small form on the couch as he passed. He circled past me, shooting a glance into the bathroom. One eyebrow lifted at the sight of my Christmas towels. Finally he stopped in front of the coffee maker, studying it as if he was going to make a cup of coffee. Or build the coffee maker.

After a moment, he turned around. His face had smoothed out. The line between his brows was gone. His frown disappeared in the neutral line of his mouth.

He sighed.

"Okay. Just this once, Noel."

Hope surged through me. I resisted the urge to bounce on my heels. My hands itched to move but I kept them at my sides. From the look on my brother's face, I could tell that even a pat on the shoulder would annoy him.

As KJ took a step toward Venir, I drew in a deep breath and anchored myself into the room. I had to be able to pull KJ out if he got caught, although with his magic stronger and more connected to the North Pole, I couldn't imagine him getting caught by this spell. It was strong but it couldn't be strong enough to catch someone still so bound to the North Pole magic.

Could it?

I could understand the spell affecting me. Ever since I'd

left the North Pole, my magic had been at a low ebb. I had to conserve it as much as possible for when I needed it. Venir's magic was stronger but even he had limits now that he was away from the North Pole.

But KJ had no such issues. None of his visits down here affected his bond or his magic. No matter how often he came, he was always just visiting. It was always temporary. His life, his job, was at the North Pole, serving Christmas and Santa Claus.

There was no stronger magic in this realm.

It should be easy for KJ to pull Venir out, especially since Venir was an ex-Christmas Elf and that part of him would resonate and respond to KJ.

As KJ reached down toward the Elf, I felt relief wash over me, loosening my tense muscles. I could feel magic tingling on my skin, the tips of my fingers, my own magic resonating with my brother's.

His hand reached down, brushed the back of Venir's left hand, and then latched on. A shudder ran through the Elf's body and up through KJ's arm. He stiffened with a grimace. His body turned rigid, all muscles tense. I could see the veins in his neck bulge. They pulsed with his heartbeat.

He'd reached Venir down in the void.

Okay, any second now he would pull the Elf out.

Any second now.

Any second.

I felt my own heart start to pound. Sweat dampened my palms. Tension itched between my shoulder blades.

Come on. What was KJ waiting for? There was no one around to make a huge gesture in front of, there was just me.

Any second now.

More seconds ticked by.

KJ stood unmoving. Frozen, like a block of ice. Locked onto Venir.

Swirling snow, had the void trapped him as well?

How could that be? KJ's magic was stronger than mine. He should easily be able to pull Venir out.

Shouldn't he?

Any second.

The pulsing in the veins on my brother's neck slowed. I watched them in horrid fascination. Throb then pause, throb then pause, pause. Pause. Throb.

Damn the halls, what was I doing just watching?

My heart thudded. My mouth felt dry, barren. My body seemed to know what I had to do before I did and it didn't want to do it.

But I had to.

I had to grab onto KJ and pull him out.

I hesitated. Just one more second.

He stood still frozen.

Too long, it was too long. He should have been able to pull himself and Venir out of the void by now. If he hadn't, he needed help.

I had to do it.

I sucked in a breath and lunged forward.

I grabbed onto my brother's left arm and yanked back.

As soon as my hand closed onto KJ's arm, I felt the hollow emptiness of the void reaching into me.

No! I couldn't let it grab hold. We would all be trapped. I focused on my body, focused on lunging back.

What was lunging back?

No, I knew what it was. I pictured myself in the waiting room. My black pants, the charcoal grey sweater. My feet shoved into a pair of scuffed runners. The waiting room itself. The sagging, brown sofa that Venir lay on. The row of yellow plastic chairs on my left. My office door on the right, leading to my desk.

Where I kept the gifts my mother had given me.

As soon as I thought of them, the stapler, the etched paper clip holder, the silver letter opener, I felt a surge of warmth and energy flow through me. The sucking reach of the void shifted, inched back. Inched back.

Back.

I yanked.

The room swirled around me. I landed on my back. Then my breath whooshed out of me as KJ landed on my chest. I felt him shaking. I grabbed his shoulders and lifted him so I could draw a breath.

"KJ, you all right?" I asked.

"What the...," he said. A cough wracked his body. He rolled off me onto the floor, landing on his side. He curled up, coughing. I could almost feel him coughing out the void, expelling it from his system. Slowly the scent of ginger bread tickled my nose.

KJ sat up and glared at me.

"Swirling snow, Noel, what have you woken up?"

"I…"

"It's a wonder you've managed to survive here," he snapped. "You keep stumbling around, playing private detective and getting into all sorts of trouble. Then you call me to come bail you out. Well, no more. I'm done."

He lurched to his feet. I scrambled up to match him. He was still shaking, his face twisted into a grimace of anger, but I could see beneath it.

He wasn't angry.

He was afraid.

The void had latched on and almost got him. Even with his Christmas magic.

KJ was right. This was my mess and I was going to have to find a way to clean it up.

Going to have to find a way to save Venir.

"I'm sorry," I said.

"You should be," KJ said. "Don't call me again for this." He waved a hand back at Venir in a dismissive gesture but cut the movement short, as if gesturing too close to the trapped Elf would cause the void to reach up again.

"KJ," I said. "Really, I'm sorry."

For a brief moment, the mask of anger dropped away. Fear darkened his eyes. His shoulders twitched forward in a hunch. Then anger slammed back down.

"Don't call me." He stabbed a finger at me to emphasize the point.

Then between one eye blink and the next, he was gone.

Leaving me with Venir trapped in the void and no idea of how I could save him.

CHAPTER

TEN

After KJ's angry exit, the waiting room felt hushed and still. Even the quiet padding of my runners across the parquet floor sounded loud as I stepped closer to the sofa where Venir lay. Closer, but not touching. I wasn't going to risk getting trapped in that void again.

But I wasn't going to leave Venir in there either.

"Venir, it's Noel," I said. "I'm going to find a way to get you out. I promise. You're going to be all right."

I couldn't tell if he heard me. His form lay still on the thick, sagging pillows of the sofa. But his left hand still clutched the magnifying glass my father had given me and as I watched, the fingers shifted and tightened again.

Could he have heard me? There was no way to know but

at least he was still connected to the Christmas magic in the magnifying glass.

Maybe KJ wasn't strong enough to pull Venir out because he wasn't yet fully Santa Claus. Even though he was more closely connected to his Christmas magic, it wasn't enough to break this spell.

Did that mean Dad could do it?

My mouth went dry. Could I dare ask him? It was already late October. Christmas preparations were already in full swing. He was in the middle of his busiest time and it would only get busier. Yet I knew he would come if I called. He would do what he could.

But I had no right to ask, no right to risk him. If somehow he got caught by the void…

I would never forgive myself.

I puffed out a breath even as it tasted sour.

A last resort. If nothing else I tried worked. At least the magnifying glass was grounding Venir. I had to hope it was keeping him in place, stopping him from sinking deeper.

"I'm going to fix this, Venir," I said. "No matter what."

No response. Not even a tightening of his fingers around the handle of the magnifying glass.

I sighed, gave one last look at the small form lying on the sofa, and *winked*.

I LANDED IN A DARK SPOT BETWEEN HOUSES HALF A BLOCK AWAY from Cameron Roger's house. Whatever was going on was centred at his house. Darkness had fallen, deeper and darker than normal. At least it felt that way. I checked my watch. It was after ten. Streetlights blazed up and down the street but seemed to only cast small circles of light in the darkness.

Houses loomed silent and still. Behind drawn drapes, I caught glimpses of light that only seemed to emphasize how dark it was outside.

I stepped out from between the houses and headed down an asphalt driveway. The air was cool and crisp. A hint of decaying leaves and dead grass lingered in the air. The world felt suspended, not quite asleep but not awake either.

Somewhere in between.

I reached the sidewalk. To my left across the street was Cameron's house. Glowing lights lit up the cemetery in blues and red, creating shadows as much as it lit up the tombstones. Even from here I could tell he'd done more work on it. There were several more creatures spread out across the lawn, arranged around the tombstones in an almost haphazard manner. But as I crossed the street toward it, I could see the effect. Move a little to the right or left and a different creature would be revealed.

Almost like they were emerging from the shadows. The effect was disturbingly real.

I reached the sidewalk in front of the house. An old fashioned, black iron fence, almost chest height, surrounded the entire yard with a gate, now closed, across the walkway to the house. Thick, concrete pillars taller than my head sat on either side of the gate. A stone gargoyle perched on each one, wings folded behind its back, mouth open to reveal fangs and a pointed tongue sticking out. The eyes glowed a dull red.

I reached out to touch the pillar but instead of the coolness of concrete I felt a roughness of something else. What was that? Was that hard foam?

Like the tombstones, the pillars were not what they appeared to be.

Fake. Hiding what it really was.

I could feel my mind churning on that like it meant something. Was it something that could help Venir? Too early to tell. Not enough pieces. I had to look for more.

And there was definitely one piece I had to find right now.

Where was Palle?

I didn't see him in the shadows of the cemetery display but I didn't really expect him to be standing in the middle of it. But he should be somewhere around here and he should have come out at my approach.

Unless he couldn't. Unless whatever had ensnared Venir with an altered home security recording had somehow captured him.

But Palle was a troll, not a creature that would be taken easily. He would fight back. I should see some evidence of a battle.

But there was nothing.

No sign of him. No sign of anything.

For the first time since I'd seen Cameron Rogers's fake cemetery, I shuddered at the sight of it. It didn't seem like such a fun display now.

Not with my friends in danger.

I headed toward the corner, pacing along the length of the fence. A soft cawing sounded, muted and low. I glanced around, then up at the house. All along the eaves trough were the dark figures of birds, standing still. Frozen.

Not real. More fakes, like the monsters.

The cawing sound was a recording I realized. Maybe triggered by my movement. Maybe something new Cameron had added today. Was that why Palle hadn't come out to meet me?

I had to hope that was the only reason.

I reached the corner and followed it around. The cemetery reached all along this side, toward the looming haunted house on the driveway. It looked so real, like a shrunken version of an old Victorian mansion with weathered-looking stone walls and a curved bay window in the front. An old fashioned lamp hung beside the door. A chain was strung across with a hand-written sign that read "Closed until All Hallow's Eve."

The detail made it look so real. Although Cameron had told me the door was a plain piece of wood, it had been stained and carved to look exactly like a thick oak door, impossible to open when locked. In the dark, it looked ancient although I knew it had to be less than five years old.

Cameron had mentioned he'd bought a new facade just a few years back.

Even the chain looked rusted and weathered. And the sign with the hand writing in red. Was that supposed to be blood?

I stepped closer and bent down to get a better look.

The door swung open.

I stumbled back. Sucked in a breath. My heart pounded. Adrenaline surged through me.

Shadows filled the doorway, until something moved. A head shifted forward.

Catching thin rays of light from the distant streetlight.

Glinting on a curve of tusk and the pale green expanse of a bald head.

I sagged, feeling my body tremble with relief.

Palle.

"Noel, are you all right?" the troll asked. "How is Venir? Is he awake?"

"You startled me, Palle," I said. "Venir is still the same but I'm working on it."

Sure. Like I knew what was happening here.

"What are you doing in the haunted house?" I asked.

"I thought I heard something inside," he said. "I came in to investigate."

"Did you find anything?"

He shook his head. "I had just entered when I heard you at the door. Would you like to investigate with me?"

He swung the door all the way open. The pale light from

the streetlights didn't reach farther that Palle's face. Behind him, the hallway disappeared into darkness deeper than any I had ever seen. I knew Palle had excellent night vision but there was no way I would be able to see anything.

"It's too dark for me to see," I said.

Palle tilted his head, puzzled. Then his brow smoothed out. "Of course, I forgot you are human. Allow me to assist."

He lifted his right hand, turning it palm up. He mumbled under his breath, too low for me to make out what he was saying but I caught an occasional word. It was a language I didn't know, possibly his natural tongue, but after a moment, I felt a prickling in the air. Through my jacket, I could feel the hairs on my arms lift as if reacting to static cling. A taste like iron filled my mouth.

Magic.

Palle was casting a spell.

In the centre of his palm, a small ball of light grew. It glowed with a soft greenish hue, growing brighter and brighter as it expanded. Soon it expanded to fill his hand, the diameter rising six inches above his palm. The glow brightened to light up the hall beyond Palle, revealing it stretching off behind him.

The troll stopped chanting. Sweat beaded along his bald head. Dark circles hung under his eyes and the lines of his face looked deeper.

Palle's magic was based in the Magical Realms and it took more effort to use it outside here in the Normal Realm.

"Thank you, Palle," I said.

The troll nodded. A bead of sweat trickled down the side of his face.

I ducked under the chain. As it brushed my arm, I realized it wasn't even iron, it was plastic.

Another illusion.

I stepped through the doorway and entered a small front room that extended to the left. In the far corner sat an old wood rocking chair. Sitting in it was a skeleton wearing a faded grey dress with lace trim at the neck and sleeves. Skeletal hands gripped the arms of the rocking chair. The skeleton's head was turned toward the door, the jaw slightly open in a grin of death.

The rest of the room was decorated like an old parlour. Faded, torn wallpaper with ornate diamond-shaped patterns on it. It looked velvet but probably wasn't. On the skeleton's left was a large, old wooden radio, almost waist high. On the other side was a scuffed wood desk. An old Underwood manual typewriter sat on top with a green desk lamp bent as if to light the keys.

Beside the desk, in the corner, was an empty wood, hard-backed chair. It reminded me of the chairs in my office.

The centre of the room was empty. Not even a rug on the floor.

There didn't seem to be anything wrong in this room. Not counting the skeleton in the corner.

A long hallway led the way out of the room. I nodded to Palle as I slipped past him down the hall. The light shifted behind me as he lifted his hand higher than my head. I heard the padding of his feet as he followed.

The hall was also wallpapered with the same old pattern, the same faded, torn look. The wallpaper only reached halfway down the wall until it hit wood panelling that ran the length of the hall. Large portraits in ornate frames hanged along both walls. They looked like old Victorian portraits but as I walked past them, they seemed to move, to shift. I stopped in front of one of a man with a thick, bushy moustache and mutton chops along his jaw. As I moved my head to one side, I saw the portrait shift, the regular image dropping away to reveal a ghoul underneath. When I moved back to the centre, the image returned to normal.

A hologram. Clever.

I moved down the hall glancing at each picture. Then I realized one of them looked like Cameron. Another like his wife, Suzanne. They had the same holographic ghoul hidden in the images.

An inside joke that most people going through the haunted house wouldn't get. I smiled. Then stopped myself. Maybe if Venir wasn't trapped in a void this would be fun.

I took another step down the hall when movement up near the ceiling caught my eye.

I stopped, staring upward. Something was down at the end of the hallway, up at the ceiling. I could almost see it moving slightly.

My heart began to pound. All the saliva in my mouth dried up. I felt my muscles tense. I swallowed.

"Palle, lift your hand," I said.

From behind me, the light shifted, upward. Shadows shifted and moved as if by their own volition, trying to escape the light. The upper walls brightened and then the ceiling.

A long rail ran down the centre of the ceiling. At the far end, I spotted what had made the motion I had noticed.

A hideous ghost, bulging red eyes, mouth open to reveal fangs, hands reaching forward with claws, hung at the far end of the hall against the ceiling. Flowing white fabric hung in tatters behind the monstrous head. The tatters swayed in the air.

The movement I had noticed.

"What creature is that?" Palle asked.

"It's a prop," I said. "I think it flies down along the rail to scare people."

"It is not real then."

"No, it isn't," I said. But from the distance it looked damn impressive.

I gestured at the ghost. "Is that was you heard?" I paused listening while the tattered fabric fluttered.

"No, it is not," Palle said. "We should continue on."

"Okay."

I moved down the hall, toward a closed door that read "Autopsy Room." On my left, I noticed one of the paintings stood out just a few centimetres from the wall. I touched the frame and the whole painting shifted. Maybe it was coming off its nail. Before I could grab the other side, the entire painting dropped, disappearing behind the wall. It landed with a bang. A gaping hole into nothing replaced it.

Then Palle shifted his hand and light spilled into the hole, revealing a tiny alcove. I spotted a tall stool and a door to the left of the hall.

It was one of the spots for an actor to scare people. Drop the painting when they didn't expect it and roar at them.

And if it was before or after the ghost prop racing toward them...

I wondered how many people made it as far as the "Autopsy Room."

I took a deep breath and let it out slowly. My pounding heart slowed a little. I had to admit I was glad I was going through this haunted house without any actors or sound effects or creepy music. I wasn't used to this kind of thing.

It was growing up at the North Pole. Yeah, that was it.

I moved toward the "Autopsy Room," pushing on the cool, steel door. It swung open easily, revealing a large, dark room beyond. Behind me, light reached through the doorway as Palle lifted his hand.

The walls looked like rusted steel. Streaks of something brownish ran down the walls. To the left of the door was a long steel autopsy table, complete with the trough running along each side. A heap of clothes lay on top but as I moved into the room I realized it was a body. My heart began to pound. It couldn't be real. It had to be one of the props that Cameron had.

But it looked so real, the bloodied head, the hands

twisted into claws. My mouth went dry as I took a step closer. Reached out.

I would not let my hand shake. I would not.

Reached.

To touch the body's hand.

It felt like rubber. Almost skin-like, but a little too thick. Silicon maybe. But very lifelike.

"Is the man all right?" Palle asked.

I almost jumped at his voice behind me but turned my sudden movement into a step deeper into the room. I cleared my throat.

"It's just a prop," I said. "It's not a real person."

"And this is fun?" Palle asked.

I glanced back at him. A frown was turning his tusks down. He looked genuinely puzzled.

"It's all part of a haunted house," I said. "People like to get scared but it's a safe place. Everyone knows it isn't real, the monsters won't really get you, but suspending disbelieve makes it fun."

The frown lines along Palle's forehead and beside his mouth smoothed out.

"I see," he said. "It is pretend."

"Exactly. Nothing here will really hurt anyone."

At least I hoped that was the case. With the powerful spell on the home security system recording, I couldn't be sure anymore.

Just another reason to continue looking through the haunted house.

"Let's finish in here," I said. "Find whatever made the noise you heard. Can you tell me what it sounded like?"

The frown on Palle's face returned. "My memory of it seems to be hazy. I know I heard something. It could have been a voice, high and wailing. Or it could have been a bird's cry. Or something banging. I...I cannot be sure."

Either it was a sound that Palle couldn't identify which was why he was having trouble recalling it or maybe Palle had imagined it, although it didn't seem to be the kind of thing he would imagine. He wasn't human and his frame of reference didn't include haunted houses.

Maybe it was some sound effect that Cameron had left on but that didn't seem likely. From what I'd seen he seemed very diligent about turning off whatever prop he wanted to have turned off.

That left only one answer.

Something was in here with us. Possibly the thing that had trapped Venir into the void.

"Come on, let's keep going," I said.

As Palle stepped into the room, I noticed a stack of cardboard boxes in the corner opposite the door. They were almost chest high with medical insignia on the sides that looked faded and old. I peered around them to see an empty space.

Probably where another actor would hide to jump out.

Along the far wall were two rows of closed drawers, like in a morgue. Glowing, greenish paint dribbled down from the tops and bottoms of the drawers, like something weird and infected was inside. As I moved past, I felt my right shoe press down on something soft on the ground. I glanced down. A black pad lay on the floor but it wasn't the only one. I noticed several scattered around.

What were they? I lifted my weight away from the pad and then pressed back down. I could almost feel the click through my shoe.

Some kind of trigger.

I glanced back at the morgue doors. Maybe one or more of them swung open and a gurney shot out into the room as a scare. I stepped back toward the table with the body and felt myself step on another pad.

Maybe that one triggered something else in the room, like the body behind me. Would it sit up?

Between the props and the actor in this room, I could imagine it would be terrifying.

In the dim light from Palle's magic, even without the props or the actors it was still pretty scary.

But no sign of anything that would make any noise. Whatever these pads triggered had been turned off.

Yet more evidence of Cameron's diligence.

"Let's keep going," I said again.

In the shadows, I caught Palle's nod. He lifted his hand higher to spread the light further into the room.

Just past the head of the body on the table, I spotted a door.

"This way," I said.

As I stepped into another room, the darkness seemed

even deeper. The air felt colder, a crisp, almost burning, cold. The light from Palle's magic seemed to penetrate only just past the doorway. I took another step inside.

And felt something brush my face.

I jumped. Sucked in air. My heart pounded.

I heard a creak as Palle stepped through the doorway. The light chased away the darkness, creating deep shadows.

Revealing a body hanging face down right in front of me.

Frost clung to his face, giving a bluish tinge to the lips and cheeks. Unseeing eyes stared past me. I let go of the breath I was holding. Although the face looked completely real, the eyes were obviously glass.

Another prop. It swayed just a little from when I'd bumped into it.

Just past it, I noticed other bodies hanging from the ceiling, some face down, others right side up. All had the same chilled look to them, white frost tinging the tips of fingers and noses. Skin pale with veins of blue running through them. Just past them, I saw walls that looked like they were crusted with ice as if it was a freezer.

With just the right amount of light and shadow, this was a terrifying room. I took another steadying breath. My heart still pounded, sending adrenaline coursing through my body. I felt so jumpy the air seemed to crackle with cold against my skin.

I shifted to the right, moving into a space between two bodies. More blocked my path. I didn't want to touch them even though I knew they weren't real. They weren't, but they looked so close to real in the dim lighting, just out of the corner of my eye.

Steady. Just take steady breaths.

The air still seemed to crackle as I shouldered my way through the room. I heard creaking coming from behind me. I glanced back. Palle followed close behind, holding the light up to try to fill the room but it only brightened a few feet around us. His expression was grim.

I nodded to him. He didn't respond.

I turned back to face forward.

At least I thought it was forward.

How large could this room be? How large could this haunted house be? It was only occupied the space on Cameron's driveway. How could it feel so huge? How could this room be endless?

With so many bodies.

I had to admit it, it was really starting to freak me out. And there weren't any actors or sound effects or music or anything.

So much for my bravery.

I puffed out a breath and saw it expand ahead of me in a cold mist.

Wait, that couldn't be right.

It was cool in here and outside but not cold enough to see our breath.

Not naturally anyway.

The crackling on my skin. The coldness in the air.

Magic.

I heard a low growl coming from ahead.

A heavy hand fell on my shoulder, gripping it. I started for a moment then realized it was Palle.

"That's the noise." His voice was a bare whisper in my ear.

The low growl came again. Not a dog or any kind of canine. Not any kind of animal I'd heard of here.

Not in this realm anyway.

I rubbed my hands together to warm them up. My fingertips were getting cold, a sympathetic response to magic, not to any real cold. I breathed in the chill air and let it out.

Hardly even crisp enough for the North Pole.

"Pretty pathetic effort," I said. "I've been in colder air during a warm snap at the North Pole."

No answer. The growl had stopped.

I moved forward, through a break between two upside down bodies.

And found myself facing a door.

Finally.

"Palle, I found the door." I glanced back. All I could see were the hanging bodies. They swayed a little, probably because of me bumping into them as I passed. There even seemed to be a bit of an air current so that probably helped them move as well.

But no sign of Palle.

He had to be in there, otherwise how could I even see anything? He was the one holding the light. He was probably just stuck in the middle of the bodies, trying to find his way out.

"Palle, follow my voice."

Still no response.

A shiver crept up my back, tightening my shoulder blades. What was going on? First the deadly home security recordings, capturing Venir into some kind of void. Now Palle, lost in a room of fake, frozen bodies.

No, he wasn't lost. I wouldn't let him be.

"Palle," I yelled. I didn't like the tinge of hysteria I heard in my voice. That just made me angrier.

"Swirling snow, Palle, where are you?"

Still nothing. I turned away from the door, facing the hanging bodies. I really didn't want to go back through them but Palle was in there.

I was not leaving another man behind.

Clenching my fists, I felt the tingles of magic swirl up my forearms, itch between my shoulder blades. Something was definitely here or had left some kind of spell behind. But I wasn't going to let it capture Palle.

I shoved my way past two bodies. They swayed, bumping into the nearest ones and starting them swaying. Soon all around me the bodies were swinging back and forth.

I ignored them. The light, where was the light coming from? That had to be Palle.

I passed a woman's body, long hair hanging down in front of her face, only one eye and the tip of her nose peeking out. That looked more real than any of the others.

Could it be real? Had whatever was befouling Cameron's Halloween display have killed someone and added the real body here?

I didn't want to touch her to find out but there was no other way. My hand shook as I reached for her arm. For a moment, the cold flesh felt perfectly real but then I felt the underlying smoothness. Too perfect. The texture underneath wasn't muscle.

Fake.

I almost sagged with relief. Thank the snows it wasn't real. Now I just had to find Palle.

The light seemed to be coming from the centre of the room, where the bodies seemed to be densest. That didn't make sense. When I had come through all the bodies seemed to be an equal distance apart.

Another trick. One that was trying to unnerve me. But my friend was in trouble and I wouldn't let such a paltry attempt to scare me stop me.

I breathed in the cold air. It really did make me think of the North Pole. Of Christmas. Of the Elves working away in the workshop, steaming up the windows with their efforts and movements. Of the reindeer resting in their barn, then frolicking in the snow when they were let out for exercise. Of my father standing in the centre of the main toy loading facility, directing the loading of toys like an air traffic controller. Of my mother coordinating the shift changes with the Elves to make sure they actually left the workshop and got something to eat and some rest. By this time of year, they would keep working until they fell over in exhaustion if someone didn't stop them.

My memories. Part of my connection to the North Pole, to the Christmas magic.

Ahead of me, I noticed the bodies swaying more. The light was approaching.

I tensed. Was this it? Was this the creature who had growled at us?

A green hand pushed a hanging man out of the way.

"Noel?"

"Palle!"

I hurried toward the troll and grabbed his left arm. My hand barely covered half of his forearm.

"Where have you been, Noel?" he asked. "I have been looking for you."

I shuddered. I didn't want to think about what his words meant.

"I'm here now," I said. "Let's get out of here."

CHAPTER

ELEVEN

I led Palle back through the hanging bodies to the door. It had the look of a freezer door with white frost crusting along the top and sides. The chrome handle felt cool to the touch and I heard a click as I pushed down on it. Then I pulled. For a moment it resisted then it swung open.

We were facing a hall with faded burgundy wallpaper with gold diamond-shaped patterns. I caught movement from the corner of my eye above us and glanced up.

A woman was clinging to the walls in the top corner. Long, stringy black hair hung down, partially obscuring her face but I could still see the bulging eyes, the mouth open in a scream.

Palle shifted behind me, making the light move, shifting it across the prop. That's what made it look like she was moving. I sighed and stepped forward. My foot landed on a mat that gave a little. Another trigger, probably to really make the woman clinging like a spider move.

I wondered what it would look like but I was glad I wouldn't see it.

I was starting to think I'd had enough of this "haunted house" and we weren't even through it all yet.

The hall curved to the right and opened up into long, narrow room. Church pews faced toward me, only long enough to hold two or three per side with an aisle leading through the centre. To my right was a pedestal where a preacher would stand to read a sermon.

But he wouldn't be reading to people.

Scattered among the pews were figures covered in grey, tattered robes. They had their heads bowed as if in prayer. The cloth hung over their heads, obscuring any features. No part of the figures was visible under the robes, not even their hands as they seemed to be clasped in front of them or resting on the back of the pew before them.

I stepped past the pedestal toward the centre aisle. There was no other way through the room but past all these pews, all these figures. I could see the door at the back on the right wall in the corner. Was it to the outside or to another room?

Only one way to find out. Past these hooded, hidden figures.

I took a breath and headed down the aisle.

The light from Palle's hand lit up the hoods and cast deeper shadows inside. Like with the prop clinging to the wall, the light's movement made it almost look like the hooded figures were swaying to some silent hymn. Then I managed to get a closer look at the figure on my left. It was sitting right up against the side of the pew, the head lifted up a little higher than most of the others. I tilted my own head to peer into the hood.

It was empty.

Only shadows. Darkness.

One of the arms was lifted up, as if reaching for the pew in front of it. I looked inside the sleeve.

Empty. More darkness.

These figures, all of them, were only draped hoods and folds of fabric, empty of anything.

That was creepier than any of the other props in Cameron's cemetery. Creepier even than the zombie in the bushes.

By the time I reached the door past the final pew, my heart was pounding. I sucked in air as deep as I could but it felt like I couldn't get enough. I glanced back, past Palle, and counted the rows of pews. Only four. Why did it feel like it was so many more?

Towering above me, Palle hunched over although the ceiling was high enough for him to stand straight. In the dim light, his pale green skin looking even paler, like a sickly yellowish-green. His lips were pressed tight together, forcing his tusks out straighter in front.

The troll wasn't enjoying this anymore than I was.

I turned back to face the door.

Please let it be the way out and not leading to another room.

I grabbed the handle and turned. It twisted easily in my palm. Cold air wafted in, bringing along the scent of wet, decaying earth.

Outside.

I breathed a sigh of relief as I led Palle out into the darkness. Our feet crunched on grass. The door led onto the grass at the side of the driveway. On my right, the side of Cameron's house stretched upward into the night sky.

Just ahead was the cemetery that stretched around from the front. The blue and red lights continued to flick on and off, highlighting different headstones and props.

I pulled the sleeve of my coat back from my wrist so I could check my watch. We must have been inside that haunted house for at least half an hour if not longer. But my watch showed only five minutes had passed.

Was that possible? Had just the suspense and anxiety of the rooms make it seem so much longer?

"Palle, how long did it seem..."

"Noel, what is that?"

He was pointing past me, into the cemetery display. I turned to look where he was pointing.

A tombstone listed to the right under the weight of an arm draped over it. Blue light flicked on, highlighting the back of the tombstone that faced us, showing the curve of the arm. Then it flicked off, plunging the area into darkness, until only the top edge of the tombstone was visible, under the weight of the bulge of the arm.

But something was weird about it.

It looked exactly like the kind of prop Cameron would have in his cemetery. In fact, there was one tombstone in the front of the cemetery that featured a zombie halfway out of the grave.

But this set up didn't look quite like that.

Especially since the bottom of the tombstone was lifted off the ground on the left side, exposing the flat wood base and the long metal spikes that had been used to drive it into the ground.

"You go around the front," I said to Palle, gesturing toward the sidewalk. I heard the click of his toe nails that were shaped like claws as they struck the concrete.

I headed forward over the hard ground.

The grass seemed to crunch under my feet. The air was chill and heavy with the wet scent of decaying leaves, turning to sludge before melting back into the earth. It reminded me to decaying flesh but there was no real flesh here. It was all fake, just a Halloween display.

Two steps. One. I cleared a larger tombstone that blocked my view. The area before me plunged into darkness as the lights flicked off. Just their regular sequence. That's what I told myself.

A blue light flicked on.

Revealing the body.

The head was slumped toward the ground, hiding the

face. From the slack position, it looked like it could belong in the display, but none of the props wore jeans and a hoodie.

And none of them slumped over a tombstone with enough weight to pull it off the ground.

This was no prop.

My heart hammered in my chest. My mouth was filled with the sour taste of dead leaves. My hand shook a little as I reached forward.

The shoulder under my hand felt real. Of flesh and bone. I tugged a little. The body shifted then flopped over onto its back. Released, the tombstone fell over onto its front.

The hoodie still obscured the lower half of the body's face. I lifted it as the light shifted from blue to red.

One of the boys I'd caught trying to move Boris. Billy Blufield.

For the briefest second, I thought maybe he was drunk and had passed out in the cemetery. But no one drunk fell asleep with that look of horror on their face. His mouth was open wide as if to scream. His cheeks were hollowed out and his eyes were squeezed shut.

I pressed my fingers to the side of his neck.

Only still coldness. No pulse.

So much for a pretend cemetery.

Things moved quickly after I called Mallory.

I instructed Palle to regain his human facade and stay near the haunted house. Before the police arrived, I woke up Cameron and his wife. They both came to the door, faces slack with sleep, blinking confusion. Suzanne tightened a silk robe around her body. Cameron wore a white cotton robe that hung open, revealing navy blue, silk pajamas. The white belt of the robe dragged on the ground as Cameron followed me down the front stairs of his house.

I led him around the front of the cemetery, staying on the sidewalk. In the still air, the lights blinking on and off gave the display an eerie glow. When we reached the spot where we could see the body, all traces of sleep dropped from Cameron's face.

"I've already called the police," I said. "They're on the way."

"Is that...Billy?" Cameron asked. "Is he...?"

"I'm sorry," I said.

In the glowing red light, Cameron's face looked stricken. His cheeks hollowed out, giving him a gaunt look and revealing the curve of the skull beneath his skin.

"How?" he asked. His voice trembled with bewilderment. "He was just helping me earlier this evening."

"I'll find out," I said. "I promise."

The police cars brought bright white lights that created a false dawn over the cemetery display. Mallory emerged from the middle cruiser, hunching in his tan overcoat. His hands were stuffed into his pocket, bulging them as he clenched them into fists.

He nodded at me.

Events accelerated.

As Cameron and I watched from the sidewalk, the officers took photos and samples all around the body. Palle and I both gave statements to Mallory, how we had gone through the haunted house on the driveway but not heard anything outside. How I had glimpsed something strange about the body hanging over the gravestone. How I had touched it and determined he was dead before calling the police.

In the flickering lights from the display, Mallory's face was a study of planes and stillness. He barely blinked when the lights hit him in the eyes. His expression never wavered as I spoke about finding the body. To someone who didn't know him, he might have even appeared bored.

But I could tell from the slight tightening of the skin at the corners of his eyes that he was angry about the boy's death.

His gaze lingered on my face for a moment before he stepped past me to talk to Cameron.

I knew that look.

He was demanding that I fix this.

"We were in bed." Cameron's voice droned behind me.

"You were having trouble with the deceased," Mallory said.

"No, it was all settled," Cameron said. His voice trembled with bewilderment. "He was helping with the display. He was really enjoying it, asking all kinds of questions about lights and different effects. He was even going to come help out on Halloween."

The anguish in Cameron's voice twisted in my stomach. Why hadn't Palle and I heard something out here? There hadn't been any sound in the haunted house and it was definitely not sound proof. We should have heard something, even the sharp cry of a boy dying.

Unless whatever killed him never gave him the chance to cry out.

I stepped away from Mallory and Cameron, heading along the sidewalk toward the far right end of the cemetery. As I passed the path leading up to the house I glanced over. Suzanne, Cameron's wife, stood on the porch, talking to one of the officers. Her hands clutched and twisted at the closure of her silk robe.

I wished I could tell her it would be all right, but would it? I didn't know what killed that boy and I couldn't even pull Venir back from the void.

They had to be connected. Someone or something was infecting this display. I had to find out what it was and how to stop it.

But how?

Normally I would ask Venir to check with his contacts in the Magical Realm. But Venir was trapped by the strange void that had sucked him in through viewing Cameron's home security tapes.

Whatever it was had graduated from disturbing fake tombstones, to ensnaring Venir and killing a young man.

I had to find a way to stop it.

I crossed in front of the far right end of the display. As before, the tombstones had been arranged in a straight line across the middle of the lawn. The lights flickered off and on, creating an almost kaleidoscope effect as they bounced off different sections of the tombstones. For a moment, I watched, engrossed by the flickering lights, listening to the low rumble of the police car engines and the voices that seemed to fade away. I focused on the lights. On the tombstones.

The light seemed to hit different sections of the tombstones in order. From left to right. Over and over again.

Different sections. Different letters.

Letters. Spelling out something.

I fumbled in my coat pockets. I didn't have anything to write with. I would have to try to figure it out in my head.

I waited for it to start on the left again and paid closer attention to the lights as they hit the tombstones. CA then it flicked to the next one. TC then onto the next. HM then to a different part of the same marker. EI then onto the next stone. FU then to the next CA and finally to another line on the same marker, N.

CATCHMEIFUCAN.

CATCH ME IF U CAN.

My stomach twisted, not with fear, but with anger. Whatever or whoever was doing this was having fun, was taunting me. There was definitely some malevolent intelligence directing what was going on. Now it was daring me to stop it.

And damn the halls, I was going to.

I turned away from the flickering lights, from the mocking sign. On the other end of the lawn, the officers stood around, carrying out their investigation, moving in a coordinated effort that almost looked like a ballet. They wouldn't find anything useful. On the sidewalk, I spotted the top of Mallory's head, his short greying hair almost silver in the dim light.

He would understand if I told him about the message, but he would want to do something and I didn't think this was something he would be able to arrest and put in jail. It was something beyond the normal reach of human justice.

It was going to have to be North Pole justice. Magical justice.

And I was going to have to deliver it.

As soon as I found out who or what it was.

I took a step forward. My movement caught Mallory's eye and he glanced over. I tilted my head, gesturing for him to come to me. Hands stuffed in the pockets of his overcoat, he moved down the sidewalk. As he drew close, I turned toward the street, away from the display and the other people.

"I have to go," I said as he got close enough.

"Noel, this is an investigation into that boy's death," Mallory said. "You are a witness. You can't just leave."

"I have to go investigate in my own way," I said. "Palle will stay here and tell you anything you need to know. He saw what I saw. Nothing of import."

"Then why leave?" he asked. "Unless you've got an idea that you aren't telling me about."

I stopped myself from turning back toward the flickering lights over the tombstones.

"I have other concerns. Venir is trapped in a magical spell and I've got to find a way to help him before he's lost for good."

The suspicious twist of Mallory's brow smoothed into concern. "I'm sorry to hear that. Will you be able to stop it?"

"I'm working on it," I said. "I'm going to do everything I can."

If he knew that I meant for Venir and poor Billy Blufield both, he made no sign.

"You really should stay and give a statement," he said.

"I'll do it later. I promise. It really won't be much different from Palle's."

Mallory's lips thinned almost into a frown. Finally he puffed out a breath.

"Okay. As long as you come in tomorrow to make a statement by the end of the day."

I nodded and stepped away, moving along the sidewalk toward the far end of the house where the shadows were deepest. Mallory watched for a moment and then turned away. He headed back toward the crowd of officers. I spotted Palle, still large and hulking even in his human form. He stood beside Cameron. He would stay and offer his support and protection as long as was needed, I knew. As far as I was concerned, he'd repaid his so-called debt to me many times over but I was glad he was still around to help.

I stepped back into the deepest shadows in the sidewalk, feeling the darkness slide over me. I was aiming for a place I'd never been, one I didn't have an anchor for. As far as I knew, no one would ever be able to anchor to it as it didn't exist on this realm. It didn't even really exist in the Magical Realm either. It was in-between the realms, in the gap between one breath and another, one thought and another. The only way to reach it was to be still, to allow.

Crisp air, heavy with the scent of decaying leaves and moist earth, filled my nostrils. I let my eyes defocus, causing the scene before me to blur into smears of blue, red, and black. I took a deep breath. Centred myself.

And *winked.*

CHAPTER

TWELVE

Hot, dry air pinched my nose. The solid feel of concrete under my feet was replaced by the unevenness of shifting sand. Darkness still surrounded me, as if it was still night but it felt like no night I had ever felt. This was a darkness that had no end. No sun would rise to banish it. It would stay forever black and lifeless.

Was this the Underwell? I had heard of it but never been here, even when I cast down a renegade spirit who had invaded the human realm. I hadn't needed to visit the Underwell to send the spirit down, I'd only had to call for it to accept the spirit but I needed to visit now.

I'd heard all the stories about the Underwell. It was a place where all old and languishing legends disappeared.

After passing the magical threshold to the Underwell, no legend could return, or so I'd heard. It was like a magical prison, a purgatory, or a hell.

No one visited voluntarily.

Except me.

All around me the darkness extended out. Dry air plucked all the moisture from my face. I felt the grittiness of the sand against my cheeks. I turned to my left. Felt myself shift along the sand, but there was still nothing around me. In all directions. Wasn't there supposed to be some kind of red beacon marking the entrance to the Underwell? I vaguely remembered seeing it or maybe sensing it when I cast down the renegade spirit. But there was nothing now.

Was I not powerful enough to reach it? To see it? Would I be lost in this strange location forever?

There had to be something I could do, some way I could contact the Underwell.

I breathed in the dry air, feeling it almost scrape against the insides of my nostrils. A minor annoyance. Not important. The important thing was to centre myself so I could call to the Underwell, ask it to reveal its entrance to me.

A breeze flickered against my skin, sending sand pinging off my cheeks. It tasted like ash on my lips. Grains of sand dug under my fingernails, scratched at my scalp, buffeted my ears.

All annoyances, all trying to distract me.

Of course, it *was* trying to distract me. If I was not worthy of calling the Underwell, it would do everything it could to prevent me from attempting it.

Had I landed in this dark, sand-filled plain because I wasn't worthy or didn't have the power to reach the Underwell? Was this some kind of purgatory waiting room? Was I trapped here?

I didn't feel trapped. It didn't have the same feel as the void spell. I realized once I started considering leaving the sand swirling around me drifted away. As if it wasn't going to impede me if I wanted to *wink* out of here. It was only going to disrupt my concentration if I tried to find the entrance to the Underwell.

I needed more power to call to the Underwell but where was I going to get it? I couldn't call upon the power of the North Pole. Whatever power I gleamed from that connection was already within me and it obviously wasn't enough. I certainly couldn't call for KJ. After asking for help with Venir, he'd made it very plain he wouldn't answer my call. Palle was busy dealing with Mallory and looking after Cameron's house. Venir of course was trapped.

What did that leave me?

Nothing.

Wait, not exactly nothing. My mother's gifts had some trace of magic. The magnifying glass from dad.

No, that was helping anchor Venir. I couldn't call to it.

Wait. There was something I *could* call.

Something with its own magic.

I took a deep breath, feeling the sand tingle up my nose. I held out my right hand.

And called for the cane.

After a single exhale, I felt the press of wood against my palm. I tightened my grip around the curved handle. Magical power from the cane tingled up my arm, making my entire body vibrate. I could feel the cane's eagerness to use its magic, a reaction to the magic of the Underwell.

"Settle down," I said. After a moment, the quivering energy racing up and down the cane diminished. It wasn't here to force anything. It was here to help me call to the Underwell.

Even as I thought it, I noticed a glow lightening the darkness to my left. I turned. As the darkness receded, I saw a flat expanse of sand stretching out before me. In the distance a red beam of light shone upward, stretching high above.

The entrance to the Underwell. It had to be.

I started walking.

The sand shifted under my feet, making forward movement slow and difficult. It felt like wading through sludge or deep snow drifts that tried to suck and hold my feet back. I tightened my grip on the cane and slammed it down into the sand.

First my left shoe lifted easier, then my right. Each step came a little easier, took me a little farther. The cane quivered under my hand, wanting me to expand more magical energy, affect more of the reality around me.

I held it tightly in check. It was almost like the cane was remembering when it used to be a faerie's staff, conveying and conjuring huge amounts of magic. But too much magic could be dangerous, unwieldy. It carried too much risk.

Especially here.

Besides, I didn't need too much, I needed just enough to get me to the entrance.

Settle down. I sent the command through to the cane, warning it that I would send it back to the office if it didn't behave. The energetic quivering diminished but didn't completely go away. It was bound to me. It would obey. But it wouldn't be happy about it.

As I drew closer to the red beacon, I saw two huge columns of charcoal-grey stone rising up from the sand. Even from a distance, I could tell they towered above my head, seeming to mingle with the red light high above. The space between glowed with the red light so bright I couldn't see if there was a door between them or just empty space.

The smell of ozone pinched my nose. Although the sand was denser, my leg muscles ached from walking. It felt like I had been walking for ten miles or more. I steadied myself with the cane and pressed forward.

Was I getting any closer? It was difficult to tell. With no other reference points, I had to rely on the red beacon and the stone columns but they were so huge it was difficult to gauge the distance.

Was this another trick of the Underwell? Another way to test my resolve? If so it was in for a surprise. My resolve was stronger than a naughty child determined to get their favourite Christmas present. Venir's freedom and the life of Billy Blufield depended on it.

Finally I seemed to be making progress. The charcoal grey pillars loomed in front of me. The red light made the seams of the brick glow on the pillars but as I grew closer, I realized they weren't seams. Symbols had been etched into the stone, hundreds, maybe thousands of them no more than a few inches tall, all glowing red from the red light. They seemed to pulsate, as if the stone was breathing.

I squinted, trying to read the symbols, but the pulsating light made it too difficult. And as I watched, it almost seemed that the symbols shifted and changed. Not in any discernible pattern but a few on the left. Then an entire row several feet above me. Then two single ones far to the right.

I didn't know what they meant, couldn't read the rough scratchings. They reminded me of my dad's handwriting. He was always too much in a hurry to write legibly and relied on mother to read it for us.

The pillars were now no more than thirty feet away and I was closing fast. The sand wasn't such a hindrance any more. It felt like I was now walking on more solid ground, possibly a rock shelf, with the sand a light, shifting layer on top.

Magical energy from the cane tingled up my arm, getting stronger and more energetic with every step forward. I breathed slowly and deeply, keeping calm to keep the cane in check. Still I could feel my heart start to pound.

The Underwell. Tales of this place warned all magic-using children to beware and use their magic only for good. To do evil meant you would be sucked down into this place and locked away forever.

And here I was. Voluntarily.

I swallowed. My throat felt scratchy from all the dust. Grit seemed to dig into the corners of my eyes. I tried to pick it out without rubbing. Showing up with watery eyes was just what I needed.

As I drew closer, the space between the two stone pillars glowed so brightly I had to squint. Through the dense red I couldn't see anything. Was there a door or was it empty? I couldn't tell. I slowed, gripping the cane to my side. It quivered against my leg.

My heart pounded. I could feel the press of magical energy against my skin, at times like a warm breeze, then like tiny pin pricks poking at me as if to test my endurance. I could feel the skin along my scalp tensing. My shoulders hunched. A headache started to throb in my temples.

Was this a magical barrier of some kind, designed to keep magic users out? I took a step forward and the pressure intensified. It definitely felt like something was trying to keep me out, trying to pressure me to turn away. I could even feel it starting to work.

A little.

But I couldn't turn away. I'd come this far. How would I ever face Venir again if I didn't try everything I could to help him? What was some discomfort compared to him being lost in the void forever?

I took another step forward.

A blast of power radiated outward from the space between the pillars. A freezing gale swept away the heat and pounded against my skin. Icicle pain dotted the exposed parts of my face and neck. It made me wish I kept my beard longer for protection. I clenched my jaw against the onslaught and felt ice crackling along my beard.

My joints throbbed in the cold. My toes had gone numb. Even as I inched another step forward, I could no longer tell if there was any more sand. The cane felt frozen to my hand.

But even as the blast wind swirled around me, I could feel a tinge of anger begin to burn. Using cold against me, the son of Santa Claus? It felt disrespectful. Insulting. Not to me but to my dad.

And I was not having it.

I sucked in a breath through frozen lips. The cold air seemed to burn in my chest. I tightened my grip on the cane. Lifted it and brought it down hard on the ground as I lunged forward.

"Enough!" I yelled. Or hoped I did. It was difficult to hear through the wailing gale of wind.

Then the wind cut off, like a thrown switch. I leaned on the cane, trying not to sag. Without the blasting cold, I could feel parts of my body start to tingle as they thawed. Within moments, pinpricks of pain began to stab me all over.

Different parts warring for attention. My poor throbbing toes. My aching fingers. My spasming back.

I forced myself a step forward, and then another. My limbs shuddered as blood flowed through them. Each step was a lurching effort. But I still moved forward.

The light between the pillars still blazed bright red. It was still impossible for me to see anything beyond it but I didn't feel the pressure trying to force me back. Had I somehow passed the test or was this just a reprieve?

I couldn't be sure. I would have to remain watchful.

I drew even with the stone pillars. This close I still couldn't discern the meaning of the symbols that shifted across the surface. On the left pillar, I spotted one that almost looked like a Christmas hat. It glowed red and then beside it another symbol glowed red. This one looked like a candy cane.

Did it know who I was?

The symbols were about six inches above my sight line. I stepped closer to the pillar. Planting the cane in the sand, I stood on tiptoes, trying to see the symbols.

A third symbol lit up on the other side of the hat. Was that a sleigh?

I was still an inch or so below having a good angle on it. I pushed up on the cane. My toes ached. My leg muscles trembled. I tried to stretch my torso, felt my the sides of my ribs begin to ache. I swayed as my body shook with effort. The red glow made me squint. It felt like sand scraped against my eye lids.

I rubbed my eyes with my left hand. Sand shifted under the cane. It lurched. I fought for balance. My feet were cramping.

I felt myself fall.

And put out my hand.

My palm slammed against the pillar.

Cold blasted through me. Red seared into my eyes, into my brain. Then I felt myself falling, and it all went black.

CHAPTER

THIRTEEN

A glowing red pressed against my eyelids. Swirling snow, the digital readout on my clock had gotten bright. I rolled onto my left side, groping for the clock with my right hand. I felt only cold stone. That was odd. My night stand was wood.

And my mattress was not this firm.

I opened my eyes.

Red light, although dim, seemed to burn into my eyes, making me wince. Three feet away was a black wall, covered with strange symbols.

Definitely not my bedroom.

Then my memory flooded back.

The Halloween display. The DVD with the spell. Venir captured. The dead boy, Billy.

I sat up and tried to hold in the groan that wanted to

175

escape from my lips. My entire body felt bruised but at least I was in one piece.

I was sitting on the floor of a small, octagonal-shaped room. The walls were black, covered in symbols that reminded me of the symbols on the pillars. The floor was hard black stone with fine golden veins that spider-webbed through it.

The air was flat and motionless. Not a hint of sand or any other scent.

I got one foot under me and pushed myself up to a kneeling position. Then I noticed the cane resting against the wall. I crawled over to it and grabbed up, using it to support me as I pushed myself up on my feet.

I shook out my arms and legs. The aching faded, faster than it should have if it was from a physical cause. Was someone affecting me magically?

"You're a quick one, aren't you?" said a voice behind me.

I spun around.

A short man stood against the wall. He hunched so far over it looked like he was getting ready to pick up a present from the floor. Round glasses perched just above the end of his bulbous nose. Thinning black hair was parted in the middle of his bullet-shaped head. A greying beard covered his cheeks and squarish chin. He wore long black robes that draped over his figure the way someone would drape drop cloths over their furniture to avoid spilling paint on them.

Although his expression was bland, intelligence glinted in his dark eyes.

I cleared my throat.

"Hello, I am Noel Kringle..."

"I know who you are, child," he said. " I am Strom-grankhaur, gatekeeper of this place. All who enter pass by me on their journey down within." He bowed lower until his hands brushed the floor. "You may call me Strom."

"Strom, I have need of magical justice," I said. "Something or someone is attacking my reality. It has trapped my friend in a void and killed a human boy. I have to find out what it is and stop it."

Strom lifted his hands and shrugged his shoulders, making his robes jerk and shiver. "What has this to do with the Underwell? We are not a library nor are we arbiters of justice. We merely contain those judged within."

"You have experience of all kinds of magical phenomenon," I said. "You should be able to tell me what I'm dealing with and how to stop it. You should know precisely how to bring it to the Underwell."

Strom's thin lips twisted into a grin. "You *are* a clever one." He pulled himself upright, straightening until the hunch disappeared, stretching and straightening his body until he towered over me. Still his robes fell to the floor, even as he straightened upward to almost ten feet. His head never touched the ceiling.

I smiled and bowed to him. Nice trick.

"Follow," he said.

He turned and I noticed a narrow door in the wall behind him. I was sure it hadn't been there before.

Strom pushed it open and slipped through, not even bending although he was several feet taller than the door. One moment he stood in the room with me, then he stepped through the doorway and was in the corridor beyond.

My temples twinged. I was getting a headache from all the magic.

I stepped through and found myself beside him in a long hallway. Reddish light glowed around us, revealing the same black stone with the silver markings. The same gold veins ran along the black marble on the floor.

I felt a sudden urge to turn and walk the other way. The gold veins in the floor seemed to almost point behind me. Answers lay that way, I knew it. I found myself starting to turn...

Strom's thin fingers locked onto my right forearm, stopping me.

"No." His voice rang out along the corridor. "He is not tribute nor occupant. He is with me."

The nagging urge vanished. I shivered and felt the cane in my hand shaking.

"I should have warned you," Strom said. "The Underwell does not get visitors as such. It is either tribute or occupant and once you leave the antechamber, the Underwell will treat you as such. Stay close to me now."

He moved forward, dragging me along as he still held onto my forearm. I followed, stumbling as he seemed to move faster and faster. Before I knew it I was running and starting to fall behind. His hand held fast to my arm until it felt like it was being pulled out of my socket.

Under his robes, I couldn't even see Strom's feet. It didn't look like he was walking or running.

Swirling snow, magic again.

Was he testing me? Seeing if I could adjust or keep up with him? Would it mean the difference in him helping me?

I couldn't take the chance of losing his respect. Nor could I take the chance that if I slipped out of his grasp that the Underwell would take me.

I tightened my grip on the cane. Trying to focus on a spell while I ran, legs pounding and gasping for breath was a challenge. I focused on steadying my breathing. Between each breath, I spoke each word of my spell.

The cane tingled in my hand. The stuffy air smelled cleaner, fresher. Oxygen poured in through my nostrils and filled my lungs. In moments, my limbs felt stronger. My footfalls became surer. Running beside Strom became easy, something I could do for hours.

Forever.

Strom suddenly stopped. I stopped beside him without even a stumble. He didn't turn his head, but I thought I saw the corner of his mouth twitch.

Had I passed the test? I doubted he would tell me.

We stood in front of an elaborately carved wooden door. The symbols that were etched into all the walls were repeated in the deep, rich wood. Swirls and lines rose and fell along the veins of the wood as if this piece of wood was chosen precisely because of how it aligned with the symbols. Or maybe it had been grown this way.

Yet even as I looked at it, I noticed that the symbols seemed to shift ever so slightly, like a ripple across the surface of water.

More magic? Or did the Underwell have its own reality, set beyond the realms of magic and human?

Beside me, Strom nodded.

"You're learning," he said. "You really are a clever one."

He released my arm, lifted his hand to the door. It swung open, revealing a deep darkness beyond. Even the red glow of the corridor did not penetrate.

"Come," Strom said and stepped through the doorway. He disappeared into the darkness.

Fear gripped me. That darkness looked so much like the void. What if it was the same and I became trapped? How would I help Venir then? How could I find out what happened to Billy?

My mouth went dry. The air felt stifling. I leaned on the cane, gripping the handle until it felt like it was welding to my palm. I took deep, steadying breaths.

It wasn't the same as the void, I told myself. Strom wouldn't have just walked right into it, would he? He would have become trapped himself, just like any other magic user. Therefore it had to be safe for me.

That sounded reasonable.

Sane.

Rational.

I felt anything but.

I felt the fear clutching at me, like my clothes that were too tight, cutting off all the blood flow to my limbs. My stomach constricted, bending me over. My shoulders hunched. My knees bowed.

Maybe if I curled up into a little ball it would leave me alone.

I dragged the cane closer to me, pressed it against my leg.

It wasn't much help to me now. No great magic in it.

But there was. The cane was one of the strongest magical things I had. But only when I was clear.

I was nowhere near clear. Not with that void facing me.

I stared into the blackness in front of me. It was like a bottomless pool of the blackest ink. But there would never be any ripples on the top of that pool. Once you stepped through, it would swallow you whole.

Could pools swallow? That seemed to be an odd thought. And pools were normally below, not vertically in front. And not with a doorway around it.

I took a deeper breath, felt the air fill my lungs. The blinding fear retreated a little.

I was just standing in a hallway in front of a large, dark doorway. That was all. This wasn't the void. Strom had stepped through with no issue. I could do the same.

I could.

I felt the fear stirring around me again, like some external entity getting ready to grab onto me. And it was something outside of myself. I saw that now. It was playing on my fear of the void, turning it against me to stop me from going through the doorway. Would I be stuck in this corridor forever? Was this the Underwell trying to trap me?

I couldn't linger to find out. If I stayed any longer I would never escape.

Venir and Mallory were both counting on me. I had to move.

I stepped through.

My ears popped from a change in pressure. The air seemed cooler, dryer. A golden glow filled the area around me, blinding me after the pure blackness in the doorway. After a moment, the glow seemed to soften or my eyes adjusted.

I was standing in a large office. Rich, woven tapestries covered the walls in swirls of brilliant red, rich oranges, and deep blues. A white stone fireplace was on the left wall, the hearth filled with a crackling wood fire. A moment later, the welcoming scent of burning wood filled my nose.

Two high back, overstuffed armchairs in burgundy sat in front of the fire, angled a little toward each other. On the opposite wall was a large wooden roll-up desk with an old fashioned wooden chair in front of it. The short back and curled wood arms were highly polished, giving off a nice sheen in the golden light.

After the starkness of the hallway and the threat of the doorway, the office was warm and welcoming. Exactly what I needed after a vision of the void.

Or exactly what someone thought I needed. Someone like Strom?

Was anything I was seeing in the Underwell real?

A chuckle rose from one of the burgundy chairs. Strom's arm draped over the arm rest and he leaned forward, gazing back over his shoulder at me.

"Quick and clever," he said. "Come and sit by the fire."

I stepped forward until I stood between the chairs. Strom sat on the right one, leaning back as he gazed into the fire. It crackled and hissed behind a metal grate.

"I appreciate you protecting me from the Underwell," I said. "But I don't have time to sit by the fire. One of my friends is in danger and a boy has already died. I need to stop whatever is going on."

Strom waved a hand at the chair. "You have plenty of time. Now sit. I will not ask again."

With a tilt of his head, he gave me a sharp look, like I was a nagging child who was about to lose the chance of getting his favourite Christmas present.

I sat in the chair. Or rather sank into it. The soft fabric cushioned my rump and thighs. When I leaned back, it gave just enough resistance and cushioning to support my back. Without conscious effort, my body completely relaxed. All the tension I had been carrying drained away. I even let my fingers loosen around the cane, but I still kept a slight hold on it. I never knew when I might need it, even here.

I glanced over at Strom. He was gazing into the fire. His greying beard looked darker and less spotty. The frame of his body in the chair looked more regular sized and I was again struck by the fact that I couldn't be sure of anything I was experiencing here in the Underwell. Everything was suspect.

But I had no other choice than to follow through now that I was here.

The fire crackled. A spray of sparks caught my eye. I turned to watch them flare up in the warm, shimmering air above the fire, then fall back down. The heat from the flames was the perfect temperature to create drowsiness and with the comfort of the chair, I could feel myself start to nod off.

I shook myself. I couldn't let whatever spell this was catch me. I had to stay alert.

I gripped the cane tighter and felt a jolt of energy. I sat up straighter, pulling away from the comforting embrace of the chair. Instead, I perched on the edge, taking deep breaths.

The burning wood smell held just a hint of cinnamon, reminding me of the fires in Dad's fireplace at home. He kept one burning almost continuously in the fireplace in his den. I had never spent much time in there as that was his private domain but I remember the ever-constant crackling of the fire with the occasional pop as the wood settled, sending sparks shooting upward. The warmth and cozy smell permeated the room, much like the fire here in Strom's office.

And that's when I noticed. The fireplace was an exact replica of the one in my father's den.

A chuckle sounded from Strom. "Not quite so quick then."

I felt my cheeks flush.

"Is this about games to you?" I asked. "Any other tricks you'd like to play before you answer my questions? Let's get them out of the way please. I don't have time for this."

Strom's head turned slowly toward me. His expression shifted from amused to stern.

"No need for insolence, child," he said. "You came here voluntarily. The Underwell tests us all. It decides in its own time and its own way. Cross it and you will never escape. Show some respect."

I pressed my lips tight together. He was right. I had come here voluntarily and letting my impatience get the better of me wasn't going to be helpful. But I couldn't help but feel time ticking away. Every moment was another moment Venir spent locked in that void. Every moment was another moment that Billy's family spent in anguish. I couldn't bring him back but I could stop whatever had killed him from hurting anyone else.

I had to.

"You do not live at the North Pole," Strom said.

I blinked at him. "That's right."

"You left to be, what is it called again?"

"A private detective."

"Yes," he said. "Yes, that's it. Tell me why you did that."

I couldn't see the point of going over this but not answering would probably be construed as being disrespectful. I was going to have to follow Strom's lead. I took a deep breath to swallow my impatience.

"There wasn't really any place for me at the North Pole," I

said. "My older brother will inherit the Santa Claus mantle when my father retires. So I came down to Toronto to be a private detective to help people."

"This is an unusual choice, is it not?" Strom asked.

"Is it unusual to want to help people?" I asked.

He shook his head. "I do not question that. I ask about choosing to be a private detective. That is an unusual choice."

"Is it?" I asked. Sweat made my shirt stick to my back. It wasn't too hot in the room but I was still wearing my navy pea coat. I want to shrug it off but I didn't want Strom to think I was trying to distract from his questions.

"It is," he said. "There are many other more standards ways to help people. Being a private detective is unusual."

I shrugged under my coat. "I don't see it that way. People come to me with problems and I help solve them. I don't have to go searching for people to help. This way I can do more."

"Is that what it's really about?" he asked. "It isn't about you wanting to come out of your brother's shadow? To show him up?"

My heart beat a little faster. I took a slow breath, trying to slow it down. Strom was trying to get a rise out of me. I didn't know why and I didn't care. I would have to keep playing whatever game he was playing to get answers. Until it was done, I was going to have to be patient and endure whatever nonsense he asked about.

And it was nonsense.

It was.

"It has nothing to do with KJ," I said.

Strom didn't reply. I could feel him waiting for more. I stayed silent, staring at the crackling fire. The scent of the wood smoke had a hint of cinnamon to it. Just like KJ.

Oh, Strom was very good. But if he wanted something, he was going to have to work for it.

"It is tradition for there to be only one inheritor to the Claus position," Strom said. "Yet your parents chose to have two children. They knew one would never be Claus, despite being raised in the same manner with the same desire. Do you not feel cheated of your birthright because of this?"

My jaw ached and I realized I was clenching my teeth. My shoulders were hunched up toward my ears. With effort, I relaxed, taking a deep breath. He was just trying to get a rise out of me. I had to keep reminding myself of that. It didn't mean anything.

Except it was working. Somehow Strom knew just the right buttons to push, knew right where my insecurities lived deep inside.

Another deep breath. I thought about my parents. They had known the tradition of only one child for the Claus position and yet they'd had two of us. I had never questioned it. Mom and dad loved me and raised me the same as KJ.

Well, maybe not exactly the same.

I remembered Mom sharing her detective mysteries with me, showing me pictures and telling me stories about the wider world beyond the North Pole. She'd never done that with KJ.

His education and training had always been focused at home, at the Santa Claus job. Running the workshop, the stables, the production schedule, the single night delivery. Laser focused.

Although I had been given an overarching review of the job, most of my education had been focused outward, toward the outer world. Preparing me.

Preparing me to leave the North Pole.

I caught my breath.

Mom and dad had known I wouldn't stay at the North Pole so they'd made it easier for me to leave. Easier for me to live away from there. But they'd never given that training to KJ. No wonder he was always so uncomfortable when he visited me.

"I don't feel cheated," I said. "I feel lucky. My parents wanted me and I got to live at the North Pole and enjoy it. But they realized I wouldn't be able to stay and they made it easy for me to leave." I glanced over at Strom. "Even if I did chose an nontraditional way to help people."

Strom stayed silent. I could feel him looking at me, studying me. I braced myself for another onslaught on my psyche.

Abruptly he stood up. His black robes swirled about his feet as he moved around the chair, crossing the room toward the desk. I had to twist in my chair to watch him.

At the desk, the thin, spindly fingers of his left hand touched a small crystal. The crystal glowed with a deep, fiery orange glow.

"It is time," he said.

A deep rumble began, sounding like it was coming through the walls. I gripped the chair arms as the rumble grew in volume. The entire room seemed to start to quiver and shake.

Strom ignored the effect, even as the tapestries on the walls began to sway. He stood tall and calm in the centre of what felt like an earthquake.

The desk in front of him began to tremble. In the fireplace before me, the flickering fire sent up shifting rays of light and shot out sputtering sparks. Under me, the chair shook even as I tightened my grip.

"Come," Strom said.

His deep voice sliced through the rising rumble that filled the room. Before I realized it, I was standing. I moved across the room as the floor bucked beneath my feet. My heart pounded in my chest. Heat from the fire made the air taste like soot.

Just before I reached him, Strom stepped past the desk to a bare patch of wall. He lifted one hand in a sweeping upward motion. In front of him, the wall cracked, a huge break running from the floor to the ceiling. Dust and pebbles rose in the air. The dry particles of dry wall warred with the scent of ash in my nose.

I rubbed my nose but it didn't do anything for the itchiness.

Strom lifted his other arm and made a pushing motion.

The wall cracked deeper. Large hunks of plaster fell away from us. White dust billowed out into the air.

Making my nose itch even more. Along with the ash, I could feel myself getting stuffed up. Within moments, I was gasping for air, breathing through my mouth which wasn't much better. Now instead of sniffling, I felt like I was choking.

Strom showed no response to the thickening stench and dust in the air. He waved his arms in front of him, as if shooing away a pest.

The wall crumbled, falling away, revealing a black hole. It wasn't even like an empty room beyond, it was as if nothing existed beyond the wall. For a moment, it reminded me of the void but there wasn't the same pull to it. It was empty. Blank.

Strom stepped toward the wall. Without turning, he motioned me forward.

"Come," he said.

Then he lifted his foot to step over the pile of rubble on the floor.

And disappeared into the blank nothing.

My mouth went dry. He wanted me to follow him into nothing?

Another rumble shook the room. The floor bucked under my feet, making me stagger. The marble began to crack and crumble. A loud screech sounded. A moment later a chunk of the ceiling fell just to my left. The chunk disintegrated into billowing dust.

It didn't look like I had much choice in the matter. I could either follow Strom into a black nothingness or stay here and be either crushed by the ceiling or fall through the floor.

Covering my mouth with my hand, I managed to draw in a breath that only tasted a little of plaster dust. Now or never.

The room shuddered around me. Another loud crack sounded above me.

I sprang forward toward the black emptiness as half of the ceiling fell.

CHAPTER

FOURTEEN

My feet and cane hit sand. Hard. Before I could be sure of my balance, the sand shifted away from me, taking my feet with it. They went one way and the cane went the other.

I fell backwards, landing on my rump.

Looking upwards.

At a huge mountain range that rose up above me like black, rotted teeth.

A dim light shone from behind them, keeping most of them in shadow. I glanced around, looking for the red glow of the Underwell, the tall pillars marking its entrance.

Nothing.

Other than the mountain range stretching off to either side in front of me, behind me there was only the expanse of sand stretching off into the distance. Even with the dim light not extending twenty feet past me, I knew there was nothing else but sand. I could feel the emptiness.

Where was Stromgrankhaur?

As if my thinking of him drew him to me, I heard the shh-shhing of robes against sand. I turned to face forward again and saw him standing in front of me.

"Are you going to loiter all day?" he asked.

Before I could response, he turned away and started toward the mountains.

I scrambled to my feet. The cane lay a few feet to my left. I moved to grab it and saw something shift in the sand around the cane. A depression began to form beneath the cane, causing it to sink into the sand.

No! I wasn't going to give it up to whatever lived under there.

I lunged forward and swiped up the cane. Then darted back.

A screech of anger filled the air and made my temple throb in pain. I took another step back. When I glanced around, I spotted Strom already twenty feet away, heading toward the mountains.

I hurried to catch up.

I could feel the shifting sand keeping pace behind me.

Finally I caught up to the gatekeeper and fell into step beside him. I threw a casual glance back over my shoulder.

"It will continue to follow," Strom said. "In case you drop your cane again. Best keep a tighter grip and a quicker pace."

He drew ahead of me. I hurried to keep up.

"What is it?" I asked as I reached his side again.

"A parasite," he said. "Sucking up stray bits of magic. When they get to be too tiresome, the Council scourges them back to almost nothing. Then it takes another few thousand years for them to get tiresome again."

"Council? What council?"

Strom's face stayed expressionless and blank but I thought I saw a flicker in his eye.

"You'll see," was all he said.

I tried to find out more but he refused to answer any further questions. And I definitely had nothing to bargain with.

Some private detective I turned out to be. I couldn't even put pressure on an informant, or someone I hoped would be an informant.

I couldn't say he was that but then again this wasn't like any other case I'd had.

Of courses, most of my cases were like none I'd ever had.

Did other private detectives have this problem? Probably not. I couldn't think of any who had to fight off goblins, renegade faeries, or possessed trolls.

The sand under our feet thinned as we reached the foot of the mountains. Slabs of rock appeared under the shifting waves of sand. A mix of dark grey that looked like slate and black so deep it was almost reflective.

I glanced up at the dark mountains above us. Maybe it wasn't the dim lighting that made them seem black.

When I dropped my gaze I noticed Strom was disappearing between two large boulders. Even as I watched he vanished. The rocks started to move together.

Swirling snow, I was going to be left behind!

I darted forward. My feet slapped against the dark grey stone. The angle tilted upward, forcing me to gasp for air from the exertion. My hand tightened on the cane. I brought it down onto the stone to gain some purchase.

A loud crack sounded, like the crack before a thunder.

Around me, the air began to move, lifting the sand in a swirling motion. Grit caked my nostrils. I blinked rapidly to keep it out of my eyes.

The wind moaned and whistled through the stone. Sand swirled upward. I could barely see a foot in front of me.

But I could hear the grumble of the boulders as they shifted again, cutting off the route Strom had taken.

Another few moments and I'd be trapped out here.

I leapt forward, shielding my eyes with my left hand. It was almost like trying to see through a snow white-out except the sand was mostly brown and the feel of it stung against my flesh.

Then I heard clicking behind me.

Rising up from the sand.

Parasites, Strom had called them, hunting for stray bits of magic.

I just happened to be one of those stray bits...

Another rumble as the boulders ahead shifted.

I'd never managed to fly like the reindeer at the North Pole but Comet had always tried to help me learn. I remembered him leaning back in an exaggerated motion, tail quivering. He would give a loud snort or even a cuff from one of his hooves to make sure I was paying attention. Then when I was watching, he would spring upwards in what started as a leap that sent him soaring into the air. But even after trying to "train" me for weeks, Comet never quite understood why I couldn't fly like the reindeer. He'd been the one to train all the others, even Rudolph, who despite the claims had been more of a loafer than teased.

Maybe I couldn't fly like the reindeer, but Comet had been an excellent teacher of jumping.

As I ran, I tensed my legs, crouched back, butt out and leapt. At the same time, I slammed the cane down on the stone. Magical energy rippled through my arm.

I felt myself sailing through the air, soaring. Higher.

Faster.

Sand pounded my cheeks as it flew past me. Then I was out of the sand storm.

Soaring straight for one of the boulders.

The space between the two had shifted to the left, barely wide enough for me to squeeze through if I was turned on my side.

But I was aiming right for the middle of the boulder. As I soared closer, I could see the angled surface. I turned my head. At least I wouldn't break my nose as I slammed into it.

Just every other part of my body.

I closed my eyes.

And waited.

And waited.

I felt my momentum shifting from forward to downward.

That didn't seem right.

I opened my eyes just before I landed.

The boulder was gone. I was dropping out of the air in the middle of a dark cavern. I tensed and bent my knees as I landed.

My feet slipped on the sand and I rolled. The sand got into my hair and beard as I rolled, cushioning me only a little on the hard, uneven ground. I finally ended up on my back, staring upward at a dark ceiling at least thirty feet above me. My body felt like a mass of bruises, worse than snowball fight with my brother.

A soft sh-shing sounding to my right. A moment later Strom was bending over me.

"Why did you see the need to make such an entrance?" he asked.

I sat up and spat gritty sand from my mouth.

"The boulders were closing," I said. "I was going to be trapped outside. A sand storm was going on and I heard something behind me."

Amusement twinkled in Strom's eyes. "Indeed. Were they closing? Tell me, how do boulders close on a path?"

I opened my mouth to answer and then closed it again. An illusion. Of course it was. But the swirling sand had been real and so had whatever had started clicking behind me.

I climbed to my feet, using my cane to steady myself. I could feel it almost vibrating against my palm.

There was magic here. A lot of it, and powerful.

With one hand, I brushed at my hair and felt the sand falling out like ice crystals. Even when I stroked my beard I could feel the gritty particles. But before I could finish Strom was already moving past me, deeper into the cavern.

I hurried after. I didn't want to be caught up in another illusion, no matter how realistic. From the aches now letting themselves be known on my body, I wasn't sure if I could survive another so-called illusion.

Around us, the cavern walls felt distant and like they were curving, leading us toward a single point. The ground under my feet was hard and as we continued walking, the sand thinned, leaving hard-packed earth.

As we reached the end of the cavern, I noticed an empty space in the wall, like an archway leading to another cavern. But as we stepped through, I saw this cavern wasn't empty. In the centre was a single square of white resting like a platform on the ground. The soft glow that had led us here brightened to fix the white platform in a spotlight, leaving the rest of the cavern in a deep gloom.

Strom moved toward the white square. I followed. As he stepped onto the platform, I saw the slight imperfections in the stone. It was a slab of white marble with veins of grey running through the surface. For a moment it reminded me of the gift wrapping table at the North Pole, a huge table where Elves wrapped presents twenty-four hours a day, operating in shifts, moving with such expert economy that even if an Elf was halfway through wrapping a present at shift change, the other Elf stepping in would move precisely into place, finger on the wrapping paper, hand snapping off a piece of tape. It was a perfectly executed ballet that went on for weeks as the presents flowed from the workshop to the wrapping centre and then to the holding area, awaiting delivery on that one special night.

I shook my head, pulling myself back to the present. This cavern was nothing like the North Pole. The bright light shining from somewhere above us made it impossible for me to see beyond the edge of the white platform but I could feel the presence of others around us in the darkness. Where they like the parasites outside? I didn't think so. The parasites had felt primitive but the presence I felt surrounding us now felt...different. I couldn't put my finger on exactly how. It felt like I was listening to different radio stations all at once, all blended into one.

Different presences, I realized. Not just one and not just one kind.

Was this the Council Strom had mentioned? It had to be.

Beside me, Strom bowed low, seeming to shrink down to the hunched size he had been when I first met him. His head almost touched the smooth white surface.

"I seek audience with the Council and request their attention," he said. His voice sounded hushed and reverent, almost a whisper, but I had no doubt those lingering in the darkness around us could hear him.

But there was no response.

Strom didn't seem to notice. He straightened but instead of regaining his full height, he stayed in the hunched, shortened form from when I'd first met him.

"I am aware there is still concern and discussion but the present situation continues to develop. It is becoming clear that it is not isolated."

A grumble rippled through the air, so deep that it reverberated in my chest. My heart beat faster as it passed. I could feel the magic crackle in the air, tickling my nostrils like ozone. Whoever was out there didn't seem too pleased by Strom's words.

Was he talking about my situation? I had a feeling there was more going on here. Was Strom using me to make some kind of point? He was the one who had brought me here, saying it was time. Time for what?

I tightened my grip on the cane. Frustration bubbled within me. I had come looking for help but was only being drawn into some magical machinations between the Underwell and some Council I'd never heard of before.

Enough was enough.

"Excuse me," I said. My voice seemed to echo outward, gaining in volume as it went. After a moment, it sounded like I had shouted.

I could see why Strom whispered.

I lowered my voice.

"I don't wish to interrupt any discussion but I need help dealing with a magical presence wrecking havoc on a

Halloween display. My friend is trapped in a black void and a teenage boy has been killed. I came looking for some answers and some ideas of how to stop it."

The rumble sounded again, deeper and stronger. The ozone sharpened in the air, prickling along my nerve-endings. I could feel a headache start in my temples in response to all the excess magical energy. I gripped the cane tighter. The energy surging around me lessened. The cane must have acted as a kind of grounding force, bleeding away the excess energy, making it easier to think even as my head throbbed.

The rumbling faded. The bubbling energy seemed to dim. A moment later, a deep voice spoke out from the darkness on my left.

"We must speak if we wish to talk to the child," the voice said. "He is unable to understand us otherwise."

"Such a primitive will be unable to assist us." Another voice, higher and shriller in quality came from the right. "What use is it to have him here?"

"He is quick and clever," Strom said. "And he has dealt with difficulties in the past."

A slight rumble started again but the deep voice on my left interrupted it.

"Words, or our young visitor will not be able to understand."

The rumbling stopped and another voice spoke from just ahead of me. The sound was musical, in an almost sing-song fashion.

"I hear tales, oh tales, of this young Kringle known as Noel. He vanquished, sent away, cast out, the goblin Red Hat, yes, I heard."

My heart began to pound. How had they heard of that case?

"He uncovered the renegade who wished to destroy the peace between the Winter and Summer Fae," called out another voice from farther away in the darkness.

"Was he not the one who cast out the spirit who enslaved the troll to cross between realms?" said another voice off to my right.

I felt sweat trickle down my sides. My right hand felt cramped where I gripped the cane but I couldn't let it go, not when my legs felt like they were going to buckle.

They knew, they knew about my cases. How? Why?

Anxiety tasted sour in my mouth. Had this Council caused the issues I'd solved? Where they behind the ongoing magical problems I'd discovered over the past few years?

"It is not us, child," the deep voice said from my left. "We do not cause problems in any of the realms. We come together to prevent them."

Reading my mind along with snooping on my cases. I felt a flush of annoyance.

"Not doing such a good job lately," I said.

Silence filled the cavern. Strom fixed me with an icy glare.

Oh, maybe I shouldn't have said that. Damn the halls for my irritation.

"You are not wrong, child," the deep voice said. "It has been of great concern to us. We have been working on the problem for decades."

I blinked, trying to peer through the white spotlight into the darkness to my left. I thought there was something out there, some figure, but I couldn't be sure.

"Decades?" I asked.

"This problem has been building for some time," said the shrill voice. "We have fought hard to contain it and done so for many years. Only lately has it spilled out into the Human Realm but there have been echoes through the Magical Realm long before that."

"How do you think a faerie of the Winter Court could be so corrupted?" said one of the voices.

"You're saying this is all part of the same thing," I said. "Including what's happening at the Halloween display?"

"There is an imbalance, one we have been trying to correct."

It was another voice from directly in front of me. One that sounded familiar but I couldn't quite place it. Although it sounded deep, it was distinctly female.

"Are you saying this is a natural phenomenon?" I asked.

"There is nothing natural about it," the familiar voice said. "It has been planned, it is being orchestrated. We have been fighting against it but still it spills out in the realms. Most can fight against it, but the Human Realm, where there is little magic, is especially vulnerable. That is why you are here."

I blinked against the bright light. I still couldn't see anything beyond the white glare, no matter how I tried to shift to peer around it.

"I went to the Underwell for information," I said. "I didn't ask to be brought here. I don't even know where here is or who you are."

"We are the Council," said the female voice. "We guard the realms and protect all life and all magic. We appointed your family to the Santa Claus post generations ago."

My mouth dropped open as shock rippled through me.

"My father inherited the job," I said. "And his father before him."

"And before him," said the voice. "But who do you think gave your great grandfather that task to begin with? Where do you think the magic at the North Pole comes from?"

This had to be some kind of trick. I glanced over at Strom who still stood in a bent position. He gazed back at me with a calm expression. I didn't detect any malice or deceit in his eyes but how would I know? I didn't know him. I didn't know any of this so-called Council. It could all be an elaborate charade.

But to what end? I had no idea and I had to admit it didn't feel false. With all of this magic flowing around me, I should have been able to tell.

I sent a quick spell to the cane, casting for any lies or omissions. The cane quivered under my palm but nothing of substance came back.

Whatever these creatures were, they were telling me the truth. The way they thought of the truth anyway.

Could it be true? Could this Council be responsible for my family holding the Santa Claus mantle for all this time?

Unease made my skin itch. I swallowed in a dry throat. The excess magic thrummed against my temples, tightening my scalp.

"What do you want from me?" I asked. "Why am I here?"

"Now we come to the crux of the matter," said the voice farther to my left. "We have need of your service in the Human Realm. Because of the limited magic, we do not have influence there. You will be our conduit."

Conduit. Swirling snow, I didn't like the sound of that. It was rather ominous.

I cleared my throat. "I'm not really conduit material. However, I will accept a retainer."

A grumble echoed around me.

"What is a retainer?" the shrill voice asked.

"We need a conduit, a vessel," said another voice. "One to hold an essence so we may see what is happening in the Human Realm."

Nope, I really didn't like the sound of that. Not one bit.

"I am no conduit," I said. "I don't give myself up for anyone. You have enough magic to possess me by force but I'll fight you if I have to. I won't make it easy for you."

Beside me, Strom sucked in a harsh breath. "Do not be insolent, child," he whispered.

The grumbling sounded again, echoing around us in ever

quickening circles. The magic in the air thickened and crackled against my skin. The taste of grit scraped along my gums. My eyes watered from the bright spotlight. I pressed the cane against my leg, bracing for a blast of magic.

If one of them or all of them were going to try to take me over, I would be ready. I wasn't going to let them make me a conduit without a fight. Venir was counting on me to save him. Cameron was counting on me to come up with answers. And Mallory would want to know who killed that boy.

I wasn't going to be highjacked into some magical mission, even if it did have some relevance to my past cases.

I would not let them make me some mindless automaton.

Mind you, with all the magic flowing around me I had little chance of succeeding in any resistance. My own magic was a pittance in comparison to the energy I felt swirling around me. I was a mere dot of light against their blazing sun. A single speck of dirt compared to their towering mountain. A measly snowflake against their blizzard.

No!

It didn't matter if they could crush me, I would not give in. I had to remember Venir, Cameron Rogers, and poor Billy Blufield.

The magical pressure vanished, like the disappearance of a sudden wind. My legs shook. I leaned heavier on the cane. The spotlight dimmed a little, allowing me to see a little farther but the space around us was dim and empty.

The Council was still there though, I could feel them pressing against my mind.

Why hadn't they pushed harder to take me over?

"We will not become what we fight," said the voice in front of me. "Much as we have need of a conduit into the Human Realm, to force you would be to become like that which we are trying to prevent."

I coughed, dislodging some of the grit from my throat.

"So are you interested in a retainer after all?" I asked. "We could share information. I can let you know what I find out." I leaned on the cane, trying to look jaunting and not like I was about to fall over. I wished I had my Stingy Brim hat. With that I really looked like a private detective.

"We will retain you, child," said the voice that sounded familiar. "And you had best succeed."

With that, the remaining magical energy vanished. My ears popped from the sudden loss of pressure. The spotlight died, plunging Strom and I into darkness.

My heart pounded. I lifted the cane to call forth a spell of light but then a soft purple glow started in front of me. At first, I wasn't sure it was real but then I saw the floor of the cavern appear. Beyond that were piles of rocks and boulders large enough to sit on. As I watched, a figure moved forward, its hand held outward. The purple light blazed forth from there.

One step, two, the figure drew closer.

Close enough for me to make out the slim figure, to almost see her face.

Who was it?

Was it Darya?

CHAPTER

FIFTEEN

I felt my mouth fall open then the woman stepped closer. Shadows from the dimness in the cavern fell away and I saw that it wasn't Darya, the faerie who had helped me stop a threat to my father, but someone who looked a lot like her. Similar black hair swept back from a pale face. Lively dark purple eyes that seemed to glow in the light. She moved quick and sure. Shadows at her back seemed to quiver, revealing black faerie wings that flexed with each step as if in preparation to open and sweep her away.

That was when I realized the carefully cultivated expression of calm hid nervousness.

I could relate.

With one smooth movement, the faerie stepped up onto the platform. In the full light, I could see she wore an unadorned dark blue tunic over black pants that were tucked into black boots that came up to her knees. She gave a cursory nod to Strom before she turned to me. She bowed her head.

"I am Talia of the House Trayborn," she said. Her voice had a deep quality and for a moment I wondered if she had been the woman speaking from the darkness. No, I had almost recognized that voice. This woman I'd never heard before.

"I'm Noel Kringle," I said.

"I know who you are," Talia said.

I heard layers of meaning in her tone but I couldn't decipher them. Was this a good or bad thing?

"You've got one up on me then," I said. "Are you the one who's retaining me?"

Talia shook her head. "I would not have called you here."

Definitely no hiding the hostility in those words.

I didn't have time to figure out her reasons for disliking me on sight. With every moment, Venir was in danger of disappearing forever into the void and whatever was haunting Cameron's Halloween display might claim another victim.

"I didn't ask to be here," I said. "I am investigating what's happening in the Human Realm, not be drafted to work for some Council. Since I'm stuck doing it and you're obviously my contact, we'll just have to get along."

She didn't respond. Her lips tightened into a thin line. The wings on her back quivered.

"Maybe they should have let you talk to a fae named Darya," I said. "She could..."

"Do not speak of her," Talia said. "I'll not listen to a word you say about her."

Okay, some bad blood there obviously. I wouldn't gain any points that way.

"Fine," I said. "Are you able to help with my friend or the problems at the Halloween display?"

Her wings stopped quivering but I still sensed tension in her shoulders. At least she didn't look like she was going to bolt or throw a punch at me.

"I would have to see your friend to be sure what spell he is under," she said. "I may be able to break it depending on what I see."

"And if you can't?"

"Let us worry about that after I look at him."

I glanced over at Strom who gave me a slight smile.

"You can't tell me what's causing all of this?" I asked him.

He shook his head. "It is not something we have seen in the Underwell. That's why I brought you to the Council, child."

I sensed there was more that Strom wasn't telling me. Why else had he been so curious about my background? But I had a feeling he wouldn't tell me unless he felt like it. Or maybe until I'd proved myself by working with this Council.

"We should head back," I said to Talia. "I've already been away too long."

"You have been away for no time at all," Strom said. "We are not in the Human Realm. Time moves differently here."

Before I could respond, he lifted his hand. The light brightened to a blinding whiteness, making me squint. Strom's form blurred in front of me. Even Talia shimmered into the whiteness.

My stomach churned and I felt my entire body drop. My feet thumped on a wooden floor.

The marble platform was gone.

The light winked off, leaving me still blinded. I blinked several times, trying to clear my vision.

A familar desk faded into view with a window beyond, revealing a darkened lot.

My office!

"Where are we?" Talia asked.

I turned.

She was standing beside me, just inside the doorway to my office. Curiousity opened her face, making her look less pinched, less angry. In the shape of her face, I could see a resemblance to Darya but an even stronger resemblance to Lekzar, the rogue faerie who had tried to destroy the peace my father had negotiated.

I was starting to get an idea of why Talia was so hostile toward me.

"This is my office," I said. I turned to look through the doorway into the waiting area. My familiar overstuffed, worn, brown leather couch sat against the wall and I could see the still form of a small Elf lying on it, unmoving.

I didn't think Venir had moved since I'd left.

I slipped past Talia to kneel at Venir's side.

His white curly hair, usually so wispy and lively around his head, lay flat and limp against his head, half obscuring his face. I itched to brush it away but I knew better than to touch him. The void would grab hold faster than I'd be able to snatch my hand away.

Venir's left hand was still curled around the magnifying glass that dad had given me. Hopefully it was still working as an anchor to keep the Elf from sinking all the way into the void.

"He has been caught in the valash mai tal," Talia said.

I leaned back on my heels, tilting my head to look up at her. "You know what this is?"

She nodded, her black hair throwing off blue highlights as it reflected light from the ceiling light above us.

"It is a powerful curse, pulling the victim deep into a boundless void," she said.

I nodded. "That sounds exactly right. Do you know how to counter it?"

Her brow twisted as she concentrated. A slight frown marred her smooth face.

"Such curses are normally cast at a specific individual. We would need to know who cast it at your friend."

"It wasn't cast at him," I said. "It was on a home security DVD."

She tilted her head, looking puzzled. "What is home security DVD?"

I sighed. This was going to be more of a challenge than I thought.

"My client created a display in front of his house. To protect it, he installed cameras, things that take moving pictures of what is around the outside of his house to deter anyone from coming in and disturbing the display."

The puzzled frown thinned on her face but I could tell that she wasn't quite getting it.Then her brow smoothed.

"Watchers?" she asked.

"Sort of," I said. "The watched images record on a disk called a DVD. The curse is on the disk but it only affects magic users. The only thing other people see is static."

She tilted her head again. "Static?"

How would I explain static to her?

"It's nothing. A flurry of grey and white whirling around the screen."

She still looked uncertain. "You did not see this static when you looked at it?"

"No, I found myself looking right into a void and felt myself pulled into it."

I described the experience I'd had in Shirl's apartment. Even talking about it again made my heart start to beat faster. I found myself gripping the cane tighter.

"And how did you escape?" she asked.

"I used this cane," I said. I held it out toward her. "It's magical and anchored me back here to reality.

Talia reached a hand toward the cane but just before she touched it, she drew back with a gasp.

"My brother's staff!" she said.

Burnt coals. I knew there was a reason why she had been so hostile.

Instead of backing away, she lunged forward again. This time grabbing the cane just under my hand.

Magic flared, coursing through me like an electric shock. Was she trying to take possession of the cane? Use it against me? But after the shock faded, she didn't pull it away from me. Instead she stood stock still, eyes closed. Her body seemed to vibrate with energy but her focus was elsewhere, elsewhen.

After a few moments, she released the cane. Colour drained from her face. She opened her eyes. Her expression looked confused by the room around her but then awareness flooded back in.

And with awareness came a sorrow that made her sag before me.

"It was true then, what they said about Lek," she said. Her voice was quiet and weary.

"Yes, I'm sorry," I said. "But how did you know?"

She gestured at the cane. "It told me. Told me how my brother subjugated and used it for ill purposes." She lifted her gaze. "It said you have not done that and that is why it is happy to be here." She bowed her head. "I misjudged you. I apologize."

"Hey, it's okay," I said. I felt a flush burning in my cheeks. Before they turned to a flaming red, I gestured at Venir. "Do you know how to help my friend?"

To my relief, Talia turned her attention back to the Elf. The black wings on her back quivered as she knelt before him and stretched out her hand over his body. I sucked in a breath, ready to shout a warning, but she didn't touch him. Instead she moved her hands in slow circles over the Elf's still form. With each circle, her wings shivered. She closed her eyes and I noticed she was chanting under her breath.

Finally, she stopped and rose to her feet in a single, smooth motion.

"He is suspended within the void but no longer sinking. How long has he been like this?"

"Almost a day," I said. "I don't really know. My trip to the Underwell and the Council has messed up my sense of time."

A slight smile flickered across her lips. "It does that. Wait, did you say a day? Not an hour?"

"Many hours at least if not a day."

"That should not be possible. He should be lost by now. An empty shell."

I pointed at the magnifying glass clenched in Venir's left fist. "That was a gift from my father, Kris Kringle. It seemed to arrest Venir's descent."

Talia stared at it and then looked at me. The expression on her face was intense and closed.

"So you are his son," she said. "The Claus who negotiated the treaty." She took a breath and shook herself. "The talisman has enough magic to hold him where he is but not to lift him out of the spell. We have to go to the place of origin to break it."

"If we go there you can break it," I said. "You're sure of that?"

"Yes, I'm sure," she said. "The magic that created it is not from this realm. That is why you cannot affect it. But I am not of this realm and I should be able to lift it from your friend."

"There's a boy who was killed, probably from the same magic. Can you do anything for him?"

"I'm sorry I cannot," she said. "If the boy is dead, he is dead. No magic I have will bring him back."

I let out the breath I was holding, a breath that seemed to have been there since I'd seen poor Billy Blufield's body lying in Cameron's display. He was gone and no matter what, I couldn't do anything about it. It didn't matter that I had a residue of North Pole magic, that I had a magic cane, that I had an Elf and a troll for my friends, or a faerie sent to assist me by some all-knowing Council. The boy was dead. I couldn't change it.

But I was not going to let it happen again.

"Venir, keep holding on. We're going to get you out of there," I said to the unmoving Elf. Then I lifted my hand to Talia.

"Come on, I'll show you were the spell came from."

CHAPTER
SIXTEEN

The air held a bite of chill as Talia and I landed from the *wink* in the street across from Cameron Rogers' house. Although it was almost six in the morning, darkness still held a tight grip, as if reluctant to give up to the anemic sunlight. But the sun should be rising soon and with it, too many people to witness what we might have to do.

I motioned Talia to follow me as I crossed the street. The lights on the cemetery display were off, deepening the shadows created by the street light on the corner. Around the right side, the haunted house sitting on the drive way was a tall slab of blackness in the dark.

As I reached the sidewalk in front of the display, I noticed that Talia wasn't beside me. I glanced around and saw her standing in the middle of road, staring up at the house.

Although there weren't any cars in the road, I didn't

want to leave her out there. I hurried back and took her elbow to steer her forward. But as I tugged, she wouldn't budge.

"What's wrong?" I asked.

"That place. It's...contaminated," she said.

The hushed tone in her voice made me shudder.

"Come over to the sidewalk," I said. "You can't stay in the middle of the road."

She followed me with reluctance. Her body felt tense, even the wings on her back were rigid.

She was obviously more sensitized to magic than I was and even Palle. Maybe it had to do with being away from the Magical Realm.

As we reached the sidewalk, a deeper shadow detached itself from the side of the haunted house and moved down the sidewalk toward us. As he reached the corner, light from the street light revealed Palle's human form. A quizzical look crossed his wide face as he drew closer.

"You have brought a faerie with you." Palle's deep voice rumbled through the air.

As he spoke, Talia finally pulled her attention from the house. She looked at him with open curiousity.

"You work with a troll?" she asked. "You are certainly not what I expected, Kringle."

I felt my cheeks flush. "I have all kinds of friends. Even some that thought they should hate me at first."

She pressed her lips tight together as I turned back to Palle.

"Where's Mallory?" I asked.

"He finished with the other policemen about forty minutes ago," Palle said. "He advised Mr. Rogers to get some sleep. The detective is going to speak with the boy's family this morning."

"How long have I been gone?" I asked.

"Perhaps three hours," the troll said. "Maybe four."

Four hours. My visit to the Underwell and then the Council meeting had felt like at least a day. Time certainly did flow differently there.

I introduced Palle to Talia and gave him a brief rundown of my trip to the Underwell and meeting with the Council ending with them retaining me. Although Palle's expression remained neutral, I caught the slight raise of his left eyebrow and the hint of an amused smile at the corners of his lips.

Who else would get a magical Council to conform to the standards of a private detective agency?

I gave him a raised eyebrow in return.

"Talia thinks she can pull Venir out of the void," I finished. "That's why we came here. She needs to see where the spell originated."

Any amusement on Palle's face vanished as his human form dropped away. A slightly pungent odour of vegetation exuded from him. It only happened when he got excited, the same reason why the mask of his human appearance dropped away in his distraction. He towered above us in all the glory of his troll self. In the dim light, his light green skin seemed a deep, murky colour. The large tusks protruding from the sides of his mouth gleamed white as he smiled.

"You can really help Venir?" he asked Talia. "You can break the spell?"

"I will certainly true," she said.

Palle's enthusiam waned. His smile faded.

Good thing as a troll's smile could be a terrifying thing to behold.

Talia didn't seem terrified or to have noticed the shift in Palle's manner. She was looking past him at Cameron Rogers' house. A slight frown creased her face as she scanned the cemetery display.

"Is this a burial site?" she asked. "I did not realize humans displayed their dead in such a manner."

"It's not a real burial site," I said. "It's just a display for Halloween."

Her frown deepened. "It seems unseemly. Perhaps this is why the spell was cast."

"It's not unseemly here," I said. "It's tradition." I gestured toward the house. "Can you feel where the spell originates from?"

Her gaze again wandered to the house. "It is difficult to pin down. The nexus feels like it is close by but I cannot tell exactly where." She moved along the sidewalk, reviewing the darkened cemetery. When she reached the corner, she turned and headed toward the haunted house.

I glanced over at Palle. He shrugged but I could see the tension in his wide shoulders.

Both of us knew there was something in that haunted house that was closer to a real haunting than pretend.

Some *thing* was in there. It didn't surprise me if that was where the spell originated from.

I sighed and followed Talia. I couldn't let her face it alone. Venir was my colleague, my friend. I had to do what I could to help him.

Even if it meant going back in that house again.

As I passed Palle, he ducked his head and then fell into step by my side. His expression was as grim as I felt. We'd both been in that house. We'd both heard the growling.

We found Talia standing in front of the door to the haunted house. Her head was tilted in puzzlement.

"This place is much smaller than all the others," she said, "but it does not hold any creature within. I feel no life inside."

"It's not real. Like the cemetery display, it's a fake house, a pretend haunted house," I said. "Although the haunting part doesn't seem quite so fake."

Talia turned away from her study of the door. "What do you mean?"

"Palle and I went through there. He thought he'd heard something so we investigated. We didn't find anything but I heard growling and at one point it seemed that I lost Palle. I had to focus on my memories of home at the North Pole."

"You did not lose me, Noel," Palle said. "I lost you."

"It sounds like a disorientation spell," Talia said. "One that would work on both of you. If you had not grounded yourself it might have led you farther astray. It is similar but not as deadly as the spell that traps your friend."

"Similar," I said. Something felt like it was prickling at the back of my mind, tingling on the back of my neck like it did when I sensed magic nearby. Some idea was percolating but I couldn't quite put my finger on it. I wanted to focus on it but I knew that would only drive it farther away. I had to let it develop on its own.

"You said you could break the spell on Venir if you came to the place of origin for it," I said.

Talia pressed her lips tight together.

"I expected something else," she said. "Something more definite. But this entire place feels...stained."

"Contaminated," I said.

She nodded. "It is like residue that something left behind."

I felt a chill clutch at my lower back like a blast of frigid air.

Residue that something left behind.

Had something broken through from the Magical Realm and infected the area? Were the contaminated security DVDs and the disturbed tombstones an effect of it?

Maybe, but it was an effect that the creature or whatever it was was manipulating.

CATCH ME IF U CAN

There was an intelligence behind it. A malevolent intelligence.

And I was going to have to stop it fast. Before Halloween

night and the thousands of children who would descend on Cameron Rogers' house for treats and thrills.

With this malevolent force, this haunt could be more than anyone bargained for.

I tightened my grip on my cane.

"Left behind makes it sound like this thing has left," I said. "I don't think it has. I think it's still hanging around."

Palle nodded in agreement. Light reflected off the tips of his tusks.

"You think it has been trapped by this display?" Talia asked. She swept her hand to encompass the fake cemetery.

"Either trapped or its chosen to stay," I said. "In a few days on Halloween night, thousand of children will come here. That's a lot of energy, a lot of life force. The very building blocks of magic. Something that manipulates magic would find that very attractive."

Palle frowned. "A few days? I thought Halloween was on October 31st."

"It is," I said.

"Then Halloween is today," he said. "Noel, today is the thirty-first of October."

"What? Are you sure?"

The troll nodded again.

I pulled the sleeve of my coat back to check my reindeer watch. It had been a goodbye present from the Elves when I left the North Pole. The black hand swept across the reindeer's body, revealing the tiny calendar at the centre of the watch.

October 31st.

Damn the halls! I had lost track of time.

"We have to find and stop this now," I said. "Talia, can you break the spell on Venir?"

"It's going to be more challenging than I thought," she said. "I need to find the epicentre." As if in a trance, she turned toward the haunted house. A dreamy look softened the edges of her face.

Of course the epicentre would be inside there, the place where I'd felt the most disorientation. As she took a step toward the house, I considered letting her go alone. She could feel the currents of magic more closely and had a better idea of how to combat it.

But she was outside her normal element, outside the Magical Realm. If that disorientation spell was still in effect and still as strong, she could find herself lost with no way to get back. She wasn't grounded to this realm, not enough to keep her safe.

She would need an anchor.

"I'll go with you," I said.

She gave a vague nod as she reached for the door knob.

"Noel, are you sure?" Palle said.

"Stay here and keep watch," I said. "Once Talia starts combating the spell there's no telling what it will do out here. Keep the Rogers' family and the neighbourhood safe."

The troll nodded. "I will."

As I turned to follow Talia into the house, I could hear the crunch of leaves under my shoes.

It sounded like the crunch of bones.

I shuddered.

Talia opened the door and stepped inside.

I took a deep breath. My nose filled with the sickly sweet scent of decaying vegetation. The crisp chill of October pinched at my cheeks. Not the clean chill of winter, but a damp cold that reminded me of the grave.

I'd been hanging around this Halloween display for too long.

And it was going to be longer still.

I stepped through the doorway into the haunted house.

CHAPTER

SEVENTEEN

The first room looked the same. Peeling wallpaper decorated the walls. The old style wooden desk with the ancient typewriter. I caught the quick glimpse with the light from outside before the door swung shut behind me, plunging the room into darkness.

My heart started to pound.

Then a flare of purplish light burst forth, flooding the room. Talia held her hand up, a purple flame flickering in her palm.

She gave the room a cursory glance before she began moving down the hall. Shadows from the light bobbed along the wall, highlighting the shape of her head, expanding it to almost cover the wall paper.

Up ahead, I spotted the ghost, hanging from the ceiling, arms reaching with hooked talons. The way the light flickered, it almost looked like the ghost would reach down to grab Talia.

My skin tightened across my shoulders and the back of my neck. It seemed almost worse to be in here after I'd already seen everything. Strange. I would have thought not knowing what I would see would have been scarier but I could feel myself anticipate each room. The autopsy table, the hanging bodies, the creepy girl clinging to the wall, the church pews with the empty, hooded robes. It was all fake, I knew that, but something about it all made my skin crawl.

Maybe it was because I'd grown up at the North Pole, surrounded by joy most of the time. We had never celebrated Halloween so it had always seemed like a forbidden delight. The idea of being scared on purpose had seemed thrilling and exotic.

The reality was neither thrilling or exotic, but gut-churning.

But this wasn't really Halloween. It was something bent on corrupting Halloween. Something infecting Cameron's display, ruining it for countless children. The real Halloween was full of spooky delights, shrieks of fear followed by laughter and candy. It really was thrilling and exotic.

This was not the real Halloween.

I had to keep telling myself that.

Talia pushed the door open to the autopsy room. The purplish light glinted off the steel of the autopsy table to her left. In the corner was the stack of morgue drawers, feet sticking out with toe tags. The way the light moved it almost looked like the feet were wiggling.

An illusion, just an illusion.

But there was something here. I could feel it. Talia could as well. I could tell from the way the wings on her back quivered as she hunched her shoulders. Her mouth pressed so tightly together her lips thinned to a slash across her face.

"You feel it. There's something here," I said. My voice sounded unnaturally loud and yet muffled at the same time.

Talia relaxed a little. Her shoulders lowered.

"I thought perhaps it was just me," she said.

I shook my head. "No, I felt it before but it's stronger now."

"It knows we are here to stop it," she said.

The steel had returned to her voice.

I said nothing. I wasn't sure if we could stop it but I didn't know if my reluctance was real or not. Besides it didn't matter. We had to break the spell to save Venir. That was real. I had to stay focused on that.

Thinking about the trapped ex-Christmas Elf helped drive the creeping fear back to a manageable level. I gestured with my cane to the other end of the autopsy table.

"It continues through that door," I said. "The room is like a freezer full of hanging bodies. In there was when I felt the disorienting spell the strongest. That's when I lost track of Palle."

Talia reached into a pocket in her tunic and then

presented her hand to me. A small clear crystal lay in the centre of her palm.

"Take it," she said. "It will keep us tethered together."

When I picked it up the crystal began to glow with a soft greenish light. It felt cool in my fingers, even the sharp edges were dull. As I held it in my left hand, the cane in my right hand tingled as if in response. Somehow the crystal and the cane seemed to be in simpatico.

I slipped the crystal into the pocket of my coat.

"Let's go," I said.

I stepped ahead of her and pushed the door open. Talia's light from behind me looked bluish in the mock freezer. The bodies still hung, looking frozen, with icicles hanging from them. White crusts of ice clung to arms and legs. Just seeing them made the air feel colder even though my breath stayed invisible.

The door creaked as it swung shut behind Talia. Her lips were pressed tight together again.

"This is when I lost track of Palle," I said. I forced my voice louder but it still sounded hushed among the hanging bodies.

Talia gave a sharp nod. "Yes, I feel..."

"Something," I said. "Can you break the spell from here?"

"I...I don't know. I need to get closer."

I pressed my hand against my coat pocket and felt the lump of crystal inside. It gave off a slight warmth. I hoped she was right and it was enough to tether us together.

Taking a deep breath, I turned to head deeper into the room.

As I pushed past two bodies, I found myself engulfed by them again. Long shadows deepened into darkness only a few feet from me. There was barely enough room to squeeze by the hanging corpses. Although I knew they were fake I didn't want to touch them if I could avoid it. And somehow I could tell the cane didn't want to touch them either.

But with them hanging so close together there wasn't much choice.

I was just ducking around a particularly large corpse of a man with a pot belly when I felt the crystal in my coat pocket begin to blaze with heat.

I spun around.

Talia wasn't there!

The crystal blazed so hot I was surprised my coat hadn't burst into flame. Maybe it wasn't an actual heat but only representative of how far away from Talia I had become.

Whatever we'd come in here to hunt had decided to hunt us.

But it wasn't going to get away with it. Not if I had anything to do about it.

I pushed past a swinging body. The space just in front of the door was empty.

But I shouldn't have been able to see it.

Something was still casting a dim light throughout the room. I glanced up to the ceiling. The shadows seemed to be coming from an area farther into the room toward the left.

I slid past a male body. The next two were too close together for me to slip past them. Any queasiness I felt vanished as the crystal began to emit a greenish light from inside my pocket. Something had happened to Talia.

When I shoved one of the bodies on the arm, I felt the rubber texture that further brought home that they were fake. Even in the dim light when I looked close enough, I could see brush strokes in the colour of the skin.

They were just hunks of plastic, carved and painted to look like frozen people. Nothing to be afraid of at all.

I took a deep breath, drawing in the scent of dust and the tang of rubber, and pushed my way through the rest of the fake plastic blobs hanging from the ceiling.

My feet crunched on wood and flakes of white plastic. The cane tapped on the asphalt floor of the driveway. Over that, I could only hear the pounding of my heart in my chest. Just ahead a yellowish light poked through the thin spaces between the bodies. Whatever was trying to hide wasn't going to be able to do it for very long.

Just another few steps.

I grabbed onto the arm of a leathery-looking corpse when the light went out.

Darkness slammed down.

The air temperature plummeted. I could feel the warmth of my breath in my mouth and nostrils. Cold air prickled at my face. My fingers felt numb around the handle of the cane. I was very aware of the press of all of those fake frozen corpses.

It didn't seem to matter much that they were made of rubber.

I gulped in air, trying to slow the galloping of my heart. Even in the cool air, I could feel myself sweating. My shoulders hunched up. I felt like I wanted to curl into a ball to hide.

No!

Fear. That's what this was all about. Billy Blufield had looked terrified. This haunted house and the cemetery display were designed to scare people. It was all about fear.

Heart-pounding, blood-curdling, spine-tingling fear.

This creature was feeding on it. Heightening it to get a better meal.

Or to gather in the energy and power from this heightened emotion.

And wasn't that void just another spell to induce the worst kind of fear? The fear of losing yourself?

"I've got you now!" I shouted. "Don't think you can fool me. Talia, are you there?"

Through the cold, I could almost hear a muffled response. The faerie was still here. It was the same old distortion spell, trying to hide us from each other.

But I had its number now.

I took a deep breath and relaxed. My shoulders sank down. The solidness of the cane in my hand steadied me. The coolness of the air felt comfortable, familiar. It reminded me of a warmer day at the North Pole when the sun would be shining and the Elves would take the day off from the workshop and run around in the snow. Dad even let the reindeer out to play, leaping and diving into snowbanks. A day like that would be filled with shouts of joy and laughter, the air carrying the crisp scent of gingerbread cookies that my mother would bake as a treat for everyone.

This kind of cool, crisp air would never frighten me.

Beside me, I noticed the leathery rubber skin of the body closest to me.

The darkness was retreating. A purplish light came from behind me.

"Noel?"

Talia's voice quivered in the air.

"I'm here," I said, making my voice boom loud and confident. "Everything's fine."

I turned and pushed my way through the bodies. In a slight open space, Talia huddled into herself, trying not to touch any of the hanging corpses that pressed around her. Even her wings quivered, pressing against her back in a way that looked uncomfortable. The purple light was a dim, burning ember in her palm, a testament that even in her fear she had been able to keep a light burning.

I touched her empty hand, felt the coldness of her fingers.

"It's okay," I said. "It wants you to be afraid. It's feeding on the emotion, absorbing the power of it. That's what it's doing here."

Awareness sparked in her eyes.

"Of course, that makes sense," she said.

"Now we have to find it and break the spell on Venir."

She straightened as she took a deep breath. Her body seemed to unfold from its collapsed shape. Even her wings looked wider and stronger.

"Whatever it is isn't here but the spell is," she said. "If I break it, that might start a cascade to drive it out."

I grinned. "I like the sound of that."

She gave me a matching smile.

"I thought I saw a yellowish light over there." I gestured with my thumb, indicating the corner behind me.

"That seems to be the epicentre for the spell," she said.

"Stay close," I said. "Even with your crystal, I lost sight of you."

She stepped closer. "Lead on."

I pushed through the fake hanging bodies, holding them back with the cane to make sure Talia stayed right behind me. She moved with swift elegance, darting around the bodies and through tiny spaces.

In moments, I reached the same pot bellied figure and pushed it aside.

From Talia's purplish light I caught sight of some debris on the floor, tucked into the corner. The plywood walls were washed out with pale blue and white streaks that dripped down to leave spots of colour on the floor. Some twigs and dirt were scattered around, looking like remnants of the outside cast off from someone's shoes.

But it wasn't simple debris. It was the ingredients of a spell. The one that had trapped Venir.

I knelt down, shifting to the right to allow space for Talia to join me. The floor was hard under my knee as I balanced. I held onto the body of the cane to steady myself.

Then the floor opened up.

Blackness stretched out around me. The purplish light from Talia's spell snuffed out. I couldn't feel my knee pressing against the wood floor or my hand wrapped around the cane.

Through a yawing, swirling wind I thought I heard someone call my name.

The wind pelted my flesh, sending daggers of pain lacing up my limbs. It was going to flay me alive if I didn't retreat.

Or worse, I wouldn't die and it would continue on forever, an agonizing fire of pain scorching my soul.

No, there was no wind. If there was, the hanging bodies should be knocking me over or bumping into each other like rubber wind chimes. The idea was so ridiculous it made me giggle.

Nobody giggled when faced with a wind that sliced open their flesh.

This blackness and pain was a defence mechanism to stop anyone from disturbing the spell. The only way I could fight it was to keep myself as grounded as possible.

And seeing the ridiculousness in things was just the way to do it.

Keep focusing on rubber wind chimes swinging from side to side...like... what else would it be like?

Christmas bulbs? Yes, why not?

Rubber Christmas bulbs bouncing back and forth as they knocked into each other. The way they swung would catch the blinking Christmas lights in a lovely pattern of red, blue, green, and yellow. Blinking like Morse code. An SOS for help.

Maybe help for someone perched on the edge of the void?

Was it possible?

I knew Talia had to be working on breaking the spell in the world outside my head but maybe there was some way I could help Venir inside here. It was worth a shot.

But how to do it?

Focus on the one thing we both loved: Christmas.

But somehow I knew that just focusing on Christmas wouldn't do it. It had to be specific to Venir, something that would connect to him, would get him to fight again.

And I thought I had the perfect idea.

I sent out tendrils into the darkness, weaving them into an image. The Elves workshop up at the North Pole. Venir had been a supervisor for the prestigious third shift before some disgruntled Elves had undermined him and caused him to be demoted.

It was still a sore spot for him. Just the thing to wake him up.

I sent out the image of the workshop, building it up in my mind. The long wooden tables set up in parallel. In the third shift room, I knew that the tables had been painted white, easier to see any issue with a toy against that plain background. Separated from the main workshop, the air would be crisp and clean. Noise from the main workshop would be muffled, with the occasional song phrase drifting through the door. In the main workshop, I knew the Elves tended to sing Christmas Carols as they worked.

But in the third shift room, they would be silent, the better to focus on the quality control aspect of their work.

Except for the time when the disgruntled Elves complained about Venir, causing a surprise inspection from KJ and the management which found a stash of broken toys. As supervisor, Venir caught the blame and was demoted. His innovation of rotating Elves through to the prestigious third shift to give everyone experience was squashed, leaving the Elves who had betrayed him running the show.

I focused on the image of the broken toys and sent it out, along with the idea that maybe it hadn't been the work of these disgruntled Elves. Maybe Venir had been sloppy. Maybe his idea to share the third shift among all the Elves was half-baked.

Maybe he hadn't known what he was doing.

I focused hard on it, using the power of the cane to amplify it, blasting it out into the darkness.

And felt a trill of anger in response.

Venir. It had to be.

Relief surged through me, breaking my concentration. The tingle of anger faded. Burnt coals, I'd lost the thread.

I refocused, sending the idea that the failure of the third shift had been all down to him. An arrogant Christmas Elf who thought he knew better than anyone else. Who didn't deserve the moniker of Christmas Elf. Who maybe didn't deserve to be an Elf at all...

The flare of rage burned in the darkness.

That's it. Come on, that's it!

I doubled my efforts. What kind of Christmas Elf deserted the North Pole to come down here? The only reason I let him stick around was the sense of duty I had to the North Pole, it wasn't because he was a useful member of the team. How could he be when he couldn't handle dealing with the third shift?

The anger focused toward me, like a burning laser beam.

I could almost picture Venir in my mind, drifting at the edge of an abyss. He hovered right on the edge between falling and staying upright. The lure of the void was powerful, a steady stream like a river, trying to pull him down. Only the small magnifying glass kept him anchored.

And his anger turned him toward me.

Come on, I sent the words out to him. *Prove to me you're worth it. Prove your idea was a good one. If you don't come here, those other Elves were right.*

His anger scorched like red hot fury. The cane shook in my hand. It amplified my magic to him but also Venir's response. I tightened my grip even as the cane bucked and jerked.

I had to hang on or the void would take Venir. Take us both.

I focused back on the Elf. He almost seemed closer. I could just make out the furled brow and the thin line of his mouth. Both his hands were balled into fists, even the one gripping the magnifying glass.

Good, no chance he would drop it now.

Is that it? Barely a few inches closer? You're just proving my point. You never deserved to be a Christmas Elf.

My words had the desired effect. Venir's lips pulled back from his teeth. He lifted his fists to his chest like he was getting ready to punch. He crouched, making himself even shorter than he was, ready to spring.

Then he was right in front of me, right fist swinging for my jaw.

I yanked my head back. Grabbed his wrist as his fist grazed my chin.

"Now!" I shouted.

The cane felt blazing hot in my hand. Pain seared my palm, raced up my arm. All the muscles in my body went rigid. I felt my jaw opening wide. My throat vibrated as I screamed.

But I kept hold of both Venir and the cane.

The pain seemed never-ending. My body shook, joints felt like they were stretching, yanking apart, being pulled in ways they shouldn't. Nerves burned, sending pain signals to my brain that overwhelmed me. I felt like I was drowning. Suffocating in pain.

Then something hard pressed against the soles of my shoes.

The pain vanished, leaving behind aching muscles.

Purplish light blinded me. I smelled the stuffy aroma of smoke. I coughed as the chill tingled against my cheeks.

The light seemed to dim as my eyes adjusted. I felt someone gripping my forearm above my cane. A pale blob floated in front of me and solidified into Talia's face.

"Noel, can you hear me?"

At first her voice sounded dim and far away, then the volume increased like someone was turning up the knob.

"Noel!"

"I hear you," I said. My voice croaked out. I coughed again, doubling over. Talia patted me on the back.

It stopped and I straightened.

"Did it work?" I asked.

She grinned. "You tell me."

She turned her head to my left and I released I was still gripping something in my left hand.

A thin wrist.

Venir.

The Elf looked pale and rumpled. His hands were still tightened into fists, one gripping my magnifying glass. He glared at me from under his bushy eyebrows.

"Ain't no Elf, huh?" he growled.

"Venir!" I dropped the cane and wrapped my arm around him in a bear hug. I felt his face squished against my waist. His breath came out in a puff. I released him and stepped back. I bumped into something.

"Sorry," I said and took a half step forward. A glance behind me told me I had apologized to a rubber body.

"Swirling snow, where are we and what's goin' on?" Venir bellowed.

"We're inside Cameron Roger's haunted house," I said. I gestured at Talia. "Talia broke the spell that was holding you in the void."

"We broke it," she said, handing me my cane. "I could not have broken the spell and retrieved the Elf at the same time."

"Wait, what?" I said. "You said you could."

"I did not realize how complicated the spell was," she said. "If you had not entered the spell it might not have worked."

"And if it hadn't worked?"

"You would have been trapped as well," she said.

"I'm glad I didn't know that ahead of time," I said.

"I wanna know why you were sayin' all that stuff," Venir said.

I turned to face him. His expression was bland but I could tell from the slight tipping at the sides of his mouth that he wasn't happy. His bushy eyebrows seemed to hover lower above his eyes. Even his curly white hair seemed pressed tighter against his skull, as if in protection.

"I needed to catch your attention," I said. "You were so transfixed by the void nothing but the most outrageous thing would distract you away from it. I had to get you angry enough to turn away from it and come after me."

"Sure," he said. "I got it." He held out his hand. My magnifying glass lay on his palm.

"This is yours, ain't it?" he asked. "I figer you'll be wantin' it back."

"Can you hang onto it for me?" I asked. "I might lose it."

The ghost of a smile flickered across his face. "Sure."

"You know I was lying about it," I said. "Well, about most of it. I really do think you aren't suited to be a Christmas Elf."

Venir stiffened a fraction. "I understand."

"If you were, you wouldn't be perfect for my agency," I said. "I never much fit at the North Pole myself."

The Elf blinked. "Thanks, kiddo."

"If you are quite finished, we should get out of here quickly," Talia said. "We have much to prepare if we are going to survive through this Halloween event."

CHAPTER

EIGHTEEN

I blinked at Talia. "What do you mean survive?"

The faerie gestured at the floor. A black stain spread across the grey surface, spreading up the whitewashed walls. Even the pale, plastic rubber body hanging closest to the area was smudged with black soot on the bottom half of it.

"What happened?" I asked.

"The spell combusted when I broke, it," she said.

"Are you all right?"

She nodded. "I am fine but in the moments before it burst, I saw the shape of what the creature has in mind. It wishes to infect everyone who will visit this place during this Halloween event."

I felt a chill run down my spine as if KJ was standing behind me, dumping snow down my back the way he used to when we were kids. If only that was the kind of problem I faced now.

"Did you see what created the spell so we have some idea of what we're fighting?" I asked.

Talia shook her head. The wings quivered on her back. I noticed the dark smudges under her eyes. She must have expended a lot of energy to break the spell. Pushing her wasn't going to help.

"Okay, we'll just have to be prepared for anything. It's going to be all hands on deck." I turned to Venir. "Are you in?"

The Elf straightened and gave a brisk nod. "You bet, boss."

"Let's go brief Palle and then talk with Cameron."

THE ANEMIC SUNLIGHT GAVE AN EVEN PALER CAST TO CAMERON'S face. If it was possible, he looked even more tired than Talia. Gone was his usual exuberance, replaced with a subdued demeanour.

I stood with him on his concrete porch overlooking the cemetery. Nothing had been disturbed for the rest of the night, as if whatever had been causing havoc was waiting for Halloween night to complete the job.

But it had already done its damage to Cameron Rogers.

He wore a black hooded sweat shirt over a pair of faded jeans. His feet were pushed into grey sneakers that might have one day, in the distant past, been white. He slouched forward, over the coffee mug he held in his hand, gazing into it as if it held his future.

"I wish I had a few more days," he said.

"Everything looks ready for tonight," I said.

"No, that's not it," he said. "If I had a few more days I could tear it all down."

"What happened to Billy isn't your fault," I said. "None of this is. All of my people are here and we're going to make sure nothing else happens."

Cameron raised his head. Dark bags hung beneath his eyes.

"How can you be sure? Do you know who's doing this?"

"We have our suspicions," I said. That was stretching it but from the hopeless look on Cameron's face I knew he needed to believe I had a handle on it.

I needed to believe it.

I kept my expression neutral and focused on projecting an aura of calm confidence. It must have worked because Cameron stopped studying me and turned to look over the cemetery set up.

"Okay, I guess the show must go on," he said.

"It will," I said. "And everything will be fine."

Inside my coat pocket, I crossed my fingers.

THE DAY FLEW BY QUICKLY AS WE HELPED CAMERON MAKE FINAL checks through the cemetery set up and the haunted house. In the darkening afternoon, he switched on the lights and replaced a few that had burned out. We filled fog machines, turned them on and watched as white, billowing clouds of fog crept through the graveyard.

If I had thought it looked creepy before, it was a hundred times creepier with the fog.

At three o'clock, Shirl showed up. Dressed in black pants under a black leather jacket, she wore her braids down. They reached almost to her waist. She stepped up to me as I stood at the corner, advising Palle to move a tombstone an inch to the right.

"Hey," she said.

I started. "What are you doing here?"

"Nice ta see you too," she said. "Had ta see for myself."

"You shouldn't be here," I said. "We don't know what we'll be facing tonight and there will more than enough civilians around with the kids."

She waved a dismissive hand at me. "Yeah, yeah, so where is he?"

I pointed toward the haunted house. Venir stood by the front window, touching up some fake moss at the bottom of the house.

Shirl marched over to him. Before he could stand up to greet her, she grabbed his arm and yanked him to his feet.

"Don't you ever do anythin' like that again," she snapped. "Not on my watch."

She gave him a hug that looked hard enough to snap his spine. But when she released him, Venir looked none the worse for wear.

Except for the redness brightening his cheeks.

Shirl spun away from him and marched back toward me.

"Okay, what can I do?" she asked.

"You shouldn't be here," I repeated. "I don't want civil..."

"Yeah, yeah, shut up about it and tell me what I can do."

"Shirl, I'm serious."

"You're always serious," she said. "Too damn serious. You gotta lighten up once in a while."

"Shirl..."

She crossed her arms over her chest. "I ain't leavin' so you either give me something ta do or I'll just stand here."

She planted one heel down on the sidewalk, cocking her hip as she settled into position. Her eyebrow lifted in challenge.

I knew when I was beaten.

I posted her inside the front door of the house to help with giving out the candy. It was as far out of the way as I could think of.

At least that was one person I didn't have to worry about. Much.

"If you're going to hang around out here, you'll need to

be in costume," Cameron said. He had changed from the plain black sweatshirt into another black sweatshirt with the logo for Woodcrest Haunted House emblazed across the back. The matching logo sat tastefully on the front left side of the sweatshirt.

"We'll get into costume," I said. "You finish setting up."

He nodded absently at me, already turning away to move back toward the front of the house. Although he moved quickly he didn't have the same bounce in his step that he'd had before.

Would he ever have it again? He would get it back if I had anything to do with it.

"Palle, Venir, everyone, come with me." I gesture my people toward the far side of the haunted house. I led them into the deepening shadows between the garage and the other house next door.

The grass was soggy under my feet, giving off the rich stench of rotting vegetation. I tried not to crinkle my nose.

Venir, Palle, and Talia crowded around me.

"Here's the plan," I said. "I want one person stationed inside the haunted house, another just outside the haunted house. The other two will be in the cemetery. Stay open to any hint of magic but keep a shield up. As soon as you feel anything out of the ordinary signal the rest of us."

"What's the signal, boss?" Venir asked.

"Jingle Bells," I said. I hummed it for Talia and Palle. "Just blast that out and everyone converge to whoever sent the call. Got it?"

Nods all around.

"Good," I said. "We have to be in costume. The easiest way for all of you is to drop your masking spells."

Alarm flashed across Palle's face.

"I do not wish to scare anyone," he said.

"It's Halloween," I said. "You're supposed to scare people. They expect it. They won't think it's real, they'll think you're in a costume. Trust me, Palle, you'll probably be the hit of the night."

As long as nothing else happened.

Uncertainly still lingered on the troll's expression, turning his mouth into a frown.

"Hey, at least you'll be scary," Venir said. "Ain't nothing scary 'bout a Christmas Elf."

"Unless that Christmas Elf is undead," I said. "Put yourself in ratty clothes and make your face pale."

Venir nodded. "I can do that."

He closed his eyes. His lips moved a little. The scent of candy canes filled the air. His image shimmered then solidified. He wore a tattered Christmas Elf costume, the red fabric dull and smudged with dirt, the white fluffy collar and cuffs matted and stained with what could have been dried blood. His face was pale and gaunt looking, and when he hoped his eyes, they looked bloodshot and fierce.

"That's great," I said. "Very spooky. How do you feel about being in the house?"

"I'm on it," he said.

"Palle and Talia, I want you both in the cemetery. Be sure

to keep an eye on the children who will be coming up the walk for candy. I'll be right outside the house, keeping an eye on everything."

"What are you goin' be, boss?" Venir asked.

I smiled. "I'll be the undead funeral director. If you'll give me a hand."

Venir lifted his hands. I felt tingling all over my body. His magic waiting for my direction. I tightened my grip on my cane and visualized a dark suit with a long, old fashioned coat, but just slightly distressed and shabby enough to look old. I imagined my face pale, my cheeks hollow with dark circles under my eyes, my hair and beard greying. Finally the tingling stopped. I opened my eyes.

"Creepy, boss," Venir said.

"See Palle?" I said. "We're supposed to scare people."

He sighed. "All right, Noel. I will be myself."

"Then I should look like a faerie," Talia said. She lifted her arms. Her wings expanded, gave a flap and lifted her into the air. Her pants and tunic shimmered and shifted into a sparkling, semi-translucent dress that seemed to glow around her. Her hair billowed around her head in dark waves. Even her skin glowed.

"That's great but I don't think you should fly around the cemetery," I said.

"Why not?" she asked.

"It might be too much," I said.

"Hey, isn't this night supposed to be about magic and scary stuff?" Venir asked.

He had a point. Besides it would definitely keep people's attention if anything else started to happen.

"Okay, just stay within the cemetery bounds. That way it might look like something Cameron rigged up."

"What about me?" said a voice behind me.

I spun.

Mallory stood in his usual trench coat with a bemused look on his face.

"What are you doing here?" I asked.

"There was a murder here last night," he said. "I'm here to make sure nothing happens on Halloween."

"Stan..."

He held up a hand. "I know the drill. It's one of your weird cases, right? And it's focused here, tonight?"

"Yes," I said. "But there's going to be enough civilians here tonight. I don't want to have to look after you."

"Is that what you told Shirl?" he asked.

I sighed. Another one who wasn't going to leave, no matter what I said.

"You can help her with the candy," I said. "If you're going to stay, that's what you do. I don't want you outside."

He looked like he wanted to protest. His lips thinned and his brows drew together. I tensed, preparing to argue, but after a moment he relaxed.

"Fine, I'll help with the candy."

He turned away and stalked off along the sidewalk. I waited until I saw him turn the corner before I looked back at the others.

"Now let's get into place. It could be a long night."

THE CROWD DESCENDED FIFTEEN MINUTES AFTER WE GOT SETTLED and the final rays of the meagre sunlight faded to nothing. By then, the fog from the fog machines had filled the cemetery with a low level drifting fog that seemed to creep across the sidewalk and into the road.

On either side of the cemetery, Palle and Talia lurked in the shadows, surrounded by tombstones and prop monsters. In the larger section that curved around the corner toward the haunted house, Palle shuffled forward, still managing to cover the entire area while looking like a slow moving monster. The dim light glinted on the tusks sticking out of either side of his mouth and off the top of his pale green, bald head.

On the other side of the split cemetery, Talia hovered as she circled the area. Her dress sparkled and floated around her, reminding me of a floating snowflake, but one in silver and blue.

I paced the sidewalk along the side cemetery and across the front of the haunted house. My cane tapped on the concrete. I kept my senses open but well contained, waiting for the slightest touch of magic.

Nothing. Not yet anyway.

It would come, I was sure of it.

As soon as there were enough children around for the creature to feed on. That's what it was going to do, feed on the children. Feed on their fear.

I knew what I was dealing with now.

I just didn't know how I was going to stop it.

CHAPTER
NINETEEN

It began first as a trickle that soon turned into a flood.

When Cameron had warned me about the crowd, I hadn't really taken it seriously. I could imagine a huge lineup for Santa, but for Halloween?

Little did I know.

Even before the sky was fully dark, the first few children arrived. Little princesses, spaceship fighters, monsters, and assorted costumed youngsters toddled up the sidewalk, some holding hands with their parents, others braving the walk themselves.

In the main part of the cemetery on the right, Palle stood motionless, looking like a large prop. Squeals of wonder and fear drifted up as various children spotted him. I heard sharp intacts of breath and saw the pointing fingers.

Then Talia drifted up into the air above the left side of the cemetery.

Gasps and giggles of delight filled the air.

It wasn't quite the same as Christmas but I was starting to see the appeal.

Cameron appeared by the side of the haunted house and strolled down to the sidewalk to meet me.

"Thanks for having the detective come," he said. "Makes me feel a little better."

I nodded as if it was my plan all along. "No problem. Everything looks fine out here."

"Yeah, a slow start but it'll pick up soon."

I glanced at the line up from the front door, down the porch, and all the way down the front walk to the sidewalk.

"Pick up?"

A slight smile touched Cameron's face, a ghost of his usual grin. "You haven't seen anything yet."

I tilted my head toward the haunted house. "How's it going in there?"

The first of the visitors had gone through. I heard muffled shouts and screams followed by laughter. The attendant at the front door, dressed in a ragged suit similar to mine, noticed our attention and gave us the thumbs up.

"So far so good," Cameron said. "Maybe it'll all go well tonight."

His voice was tight with strain. His smile looked pained. He had the look of a man trying to convince himself of a desired outcome but not believing it. He needed me to affirm it for him. And damn the halls if I wasn't going to do that.

"It's going to be fine," I said. "My team will make sure of it."

The squint lines around his eyes faded. His smile looked a little more genuine.

"You think so?" he asked.

I nodded. "We're professionals. We handle things like this all the time."

He let out a deep breath. "I'm glad you're here." He patted my shoulder. "Try not to get trampled by the crowd."

He moved away before I could comment. When I turned back to face the street, I was starting to see what he meant.

More and more people were converging on the house. The sound of their voices filled the air with chatter and laughter. Older children in costume darted away from their parents, racing toward the front walk to get in line for candy or headed toward the haunted house. A line stretched down the street, away from the house.

I was starting to understand the magnitude of what Cameron had been talking about.

And it was just going to make things more difficult.

No, more challenging. I had to keep a positive attitude about it. That was the only thing that would get me through. Especially if it was what I thought it was.

I was going to need all the positivity I could get.

Darkness settled over the neighbourhood. The fog thickened, spreading out from the cemetery, across the sidewalks and spilling on to the street. It crept along the ground, rising only to knee height on me but that meant it was almost shoulder deep for the youngest toddlers.

I watched as they soldiered up the front walk toward the door, the thick, white fog almost obscuring their costumes. They looked like they were wading through a sea of white.

I didn't like the look of it at all.

This was no ordinary fog.

I tilted my head, catching Palle's gaze. I gave a nod toward the front walk. He dipped his head in acknowledgement then turned to head toward the porch. He moved slowly, probably trying not to scare the kids.

I heard only giggles and squeals.

So far so good.

On the other side of the cemetery, Talia caught Palle's movement. She tilted her head and pointed at herself. I gave her a nod. She started to float across the cemetery toward the front walk.

More squeals. More giggles.

Maybe we would be able to cover things after all.

Then I heard a startled shout from behind me.

I spun.

Out of the corner of my eye, I caught a glimpse of a flailing arm, then it vanished beneath the fog. A woman in a grey, puffy jacket was waving her arms at the fog in front of her.

The crowd had grown so large it had spilled out into the street, almost reaching the sidewalk on the other side. I knew now why Cameron paid the city to have the street blocked off. The crowd was a sea of people.

In the middle of it, I saw the woman struggling.

"Jeremy?" Her shout reached me over the general chatter. "Jeremy!"

I slipped through the crowd toward her. Her shouts became more frantic. Her head whipped from side to side as she battered at the fog. Around her, a few people were starting to notice. Murmurs of concern started.

Within moments, I reached her side. I touched her elbow to get her attention.

"Can I help you, ma'm?" I asked.

"My son, Jeremy, he was right here," she said. "Right here and now he's gone." Her voice rose in volume. "He's gone!"

"I'm sure he's around here somewhere," I said. I kept my voice low and soothing. At the same time, I focused on her, sending out waves of soothing support. It was tinged with a Christmas feel but at least I knew it would calm her.

Her rapid breathing slowed and became less ragged. Her gaze fixed on me.

"We'll find him," I said and sent another blast of calm toward her.

"You think so?" she asked. Her voice trembled a little but otherwise sounded normal.

"I know so," I said. "Let's all look."

I turned to the man on my left. He wore a navy coat with a knit cap pulled over his ears.

"We're looking for a boy named Jeremy," I said. "Can you

help us?" I turned back to the woman. "What was his costume?"

"He was a ninja," she said.

"Looks like he's getting some great practice," I said.

She gave a weak laugh as I turned back to the man.

"Can you help us find Jeremy the ninja?" I raised my voice, turning to encompass the people surrounding us. I focused on a wave of good fellowship. Impassive expressions softened. Several people stepped forward.

"I'll help."

"Where was he last?"

"Did he run off?"

Soon a large circle of people around the woman were talking and looking around. A shout sounded about ten feet away, almost in the middle of the street. A man with a shaved head, wearing a jean jacket had his hand wrapped around the forearm of a boy dressed all in black with a black bandana tied around his blond hair.

"Is this the ninja?" the man called.

"Jeremy!" The woman shoved her way through the crowd. It parted, leaving a clear path for her to the boy. I followed in her wake.

The woman reached the boy and pulled him into an embrace. The boy's face was squished into her shoulder but not before I could see his slightly annoyed expression.

"C'mon, mom," he said. "I was goin' for some candy. I had to get some before they ran out."

I caught a hint of panic in his voice.

"There's plenty of candy," I said. "There's no chance they'll run out before you get some."

Uncertainty crossed his face as he pulled back from his mother.

"Really?" he asked.

"Of course, they have tons of it."

I smiled, letting my smoothing effort flow toward him. The boy relaxed. He smiled up at his mother.

"Sorry, mom, I was tryin' to get in line for the candy. I was afraid they were gonna run out."

"Let's get in line then," the woman said. She kept her arm around his shoulder as she started to steer him through the crowd toward the front of the house.

Afraid he would miss out on the candy.

Fear.

I was sure now. I knew what it was.

A Phobophagus, the Fear Eater. It fed on the emotion of fear. The stronger the emotion, the more it fed and the stronger it got.

And what better place to get a massive dose of it than at a Halloween haunt?

How could I fight this? The whole point of the haunt was to scare people.

But it was to scare people for fun, not to really scare them. Not the way the Fear Eater wanted. But it could work with it.

I had to find a way to keep the fun stronger than the fear.

Then I had to find the Phobophagus and banish it.

Phobophagus were shifters. It could be in any form, any disguise. But I should be able to detect its magic when I saw it.

I had to tell the others.

The fog had thickened and seemed to absorb the light. As I slid through the crowd, heading for the front of the cemetery, I heard a slight pop. The corner street light flared and winked out. The darkness deepened. Still the pinprick lights in the cemetery glowed strong.

The Phobophagus might want to get rid of the light to create fear but the cemetery lights highlighted monsters and tombstones. Maybe it would hesitate in destroying them.

As I passed the corner, one of the green lights pointing at a tombstone winked out.

So much for hesitation.

The air seemed to crackle with ozone. I stilled myself and focused. Not just ozone, it was an aftereffect of magic but too dispersed for me to target the user.

The Phobophagus knew I was hunting it and was doing a good job of hiding.

Too good a job.

I reached the front of the fence. The line up the front walk was jammed with kids, all giggling and joshing each other. As I watched, it moved steadily but never seemed to get any shorter.

Palle stood near the fence, closer to the porch. I could tell from the movement of his head that he was scanning the line. As his head turned toward me, I gestured him toward me. Slowly, he turned and ambled toward me. As he moved, I heard an excited mumble run through the line.

They had thought he was a prop.

Palle reached the fence and ducked his head toward me. "Noel?"

"It's a Phobophagus," I said. "A Fear Eater. Tell Talia and see if you can let Shirl and Stan know. We have to keep the scares fun."

"And Venir?" he asked.

"I'll tell Venir," I said. "The Phobophagus has already started to affect the lights and the fog. It's setting the stage to generate a massive amount of fear. We have to stop it."

The troll nodded. "I will ready the others."

He turned away, heading back up toward the porch. He waved toward Talia who floated higher into the air. A murmur ran through the line then grew in volume as the faerie drifted above them toward the troll. As she descended, I turned away and headed for the haunted house.

I could trust Palle to warn them properly. I had to get to Venir.

The crowd had thickened, packing tighter together, making it difficult to move. I pushed my way through, darting into gaps just before they closed. The air buzzed with voices, adults talking, children laughing, giggling, or squealing with delight.

I reached the side of the haunted house, near the exit door. Which way was the fastest to get to Venir? Probably through the front but that would mean cutting into the line.

If I went through the back way, I might be able to avoid any of the customers walking through.

I waited until the door opened and a couple almost fell out. The woman was laughing and the man was shaking his head, repeating, "I was not."

Just before the door closed, I grabbed it and slipped inside.

Here I went again. Back into the haunted house.

CHAPTER

TWENTY

Pale blue light lit up the false chapel. The dark, wooden pews faced away from me, toward the opening where the next set of people would come in. At the podium at the front was a tall man dressed in black robes. His face was painted to look like a skull. A tall, black coned hat sat on his head and he clasped a staff with a skull on top.

"Hey, you're supposed to go through the front," he said.

"Security," I said. "I work for Cameron Rogers. Have you noticed anything odd in here?"

The man shrugged, jostling the robes.

"Screaming kids, laughing adults, and vice versa. All normal."

I nodded. "Great. Keep an eye out. There's someone that wants to really scare people and not in a fun way. In a terrify

273

them to death way. If someone like that comes around or you feel strange in any way, just start laughing and joking with the customers. We're here to scare them but to make it fun too."

"Okay. I'll watch out."

For a moment, the man's voice sounded younger, almost like a young boy. I smiled at him and could feel him relax.

A shout sounded from the room beyond.

"That's the next group," the man said. "Go stand by the wall out of the way."

I darted past the pews and pressed myself against the wall. I folded my hands, holding the cane in front of me and bowed my head. With my ragged clothes, scuffed top hat, and makeup, I almost fit in.

Giggling sounded, then two adults and two children shuffled through the doorway. A woman wearing a white puffy coat came first, hanging onto the shoulders of a boy in front of her. He had pieces of coloured cardboard attached to him, making him look like some kind of robot. Behind them, a man wearing a leather jacket came. He carried a young girl dressed as a witch in his arms. She had her arms wrapped around his neck, her face buried in his shoulder. Even over the howling, creepy music, I could hear her whimpering.

Scared. And not in a fun way.

But in the way that would satisfy, and even call to, the Phobophagus.

As they passed the podium, the man dressed as a demented preacher started screeching. The girl tightened her grip on the man's neck even as the others screamed and chuckled.

She lifted her head, just an inch, and opened one eye.

Looking right at me.

I smiled at her. And thought of Christmas. The sparkling lights. The crisp cold, driven away by a warm hearth and the warmer hugs from parents. Tasty hot cocoa and sweet sugar cookies with crushed candy cane sprinkled on top. The excitement of waiting for Santa, of waiting to open presents.

I put it all into my smile.

The little girl lifted her face, gasping. The man tightened his grip around her.

"It's okay, Sally bear," he said.

The girl stared at me, eyes wide with wonder.

"Santa...," she breathed.

The man chuckled and rubbed her back. "Not yet, sweetie."

I held a finger to my lips.

The girl pressed her lips tight together and then giggled.

She pressed her face back into the man's shoulder but this time kept her head turned so she could see.

And she kept giggling.

I breathed a sigh of relief as they hurried down the aisle between the pews and out the door. Their laughter and shouts mingled with the music and faded away.

"Best reaction of the night," said the man in the black robes. "You should stay here, man, and we can double time them."

"Maybe later," I said. "I have to finish inspecting the rest of the haunt."

He nodded. "You can head out now. I don't think the next group in coming for a few minutes."

I turned the corner, leaving the chapel behind. A few steps beyond was the door to the fake cold storage area with the hanging bodies. I took a deep breath, steeling myself. The creepy music seemed to swell in volume. Despite the chill, I felt myself sweating under the tattered coat.

A touch of fear tickled the base of my spine.

No! Even if I was entering the room where it had done its spell, I wasn't going to let the Phobophagus win. I squared my shoulders. The creepy Halloween music was just like this holiday's Jingle Bells. Festive music celebrating the day. Nothing else.

All of this, the haunted house, the cemetery display, all of it was to celebrate a festive day.

I pulled the door open and stepped through.

Cold blue light made the bodies seem to sway even before I pushed through. My heart began to pound a little. Just from exertion. That was all. Nothing to fear here. Every body was just a plastic dummy.

Never mind that this room seemed to be the heart of where the Phobophagus was striking from.

A good choice. A room of hanging bodies was certainly one that would scare most people. But I'd been here enough times that it didn't scare me. Not even a little bit.

Then a body on my right moved.

I hadn't touched it. Hadn't come near it. I was heading straight through for the door back into the morgue room.

But the body moved.

A trick of the light, that was all. I took a deeper breath, aware that my heart was still beating too fast. My body felt too tense, too ready to jump.

Everything was plastic in here. Nothing real. Just pretend.

Then the body swayed again.

A head poked out from behind it.

A girl with dark hair slicked back from her forehead and her face painted white with light blue highlights, making her look frozen.

"You're comin' from the wrong direction," she said.

I let go of my breath. Another actor. Of course there would be one in this room.

"I work for Cameron," I said. "There's someone who is trying to scare people in a bad way. I checking through to make sure everyone keeps a look out for him."

The girl nodded. "What's he look like?"

"I'm not sure," I said. "Just watch for anything unusual. Keep the scares fun. If someone gets too scared, make sure you reassure them."

A frown creased her makeup. "That's not what Cameron told us."

"New orders," I said. "We want to keep it fun and scary but not too scary."

She shrugged. "Okay."

"I need to get to the morgue room. A short man dressed like an undead Christmas Elf is supposed to be in there."

"Go a little more that way." She pointed toward the right. "The door is in the corner." She cocked her head. "Sounds clear but you should hurry. Another group'll be coming through any time."

"Thanks," I said.

The girl retreated. Soon the bodies covered her, making it impossible to tell where she was.

Definitely a good scare.

I just hoped it remained that way.

I angled toward the right, in the direction the girl had pointed out. I pushed past four more rows of bodies before I found the door.

Just as I reached for it, I felt the temperature in the room plummet. In the dim blue light, my breath came out like a white fog. A moment later, I heard a scream rise over the creepy music.

The girl in the white makeup.

I spun toward the sound but the bodies made it difficult to tell where it had come from. For a moment, I hesitated. What if the Phobophagus had pulled her into the void? How could I fight that on my own? I tightened my grip on my cane and felt it tingle against my palm in response, magic at the ready.

The scream faded, covered by the creepy music intoning deep, melodic tones. I could just turn back around and find

Venir in the morgue. What was one girl in white makeup? I didn't even know her name.

Why bother?

I shook my head. Those thoughts, they weren't mine. I could feel them pressing against me, trying to steer me away.

No chance.

I plunged back into the room, shoving bodies out of the way. They swung back and forth, knocking into others, sending then swaying. Soon it seemed like the entire room was moving.

I angled toward the left, where I thought the girl had come from. She had probably been standing in a corner, ready to jump out at people.

I smelled a thickening ozone scent, the telltale trace of magic. The Phobophagus. My heart pounded. The cane felt slick against my palm. I was sweating. Nervous.

Afraid.

I had to fight against it. I couldn't let the Phobophagus take her. She would be the first of many.

And not just at this Halloween display.

This was the opening gambit of a much bigger game and I couldn't let it win.

I shoved my way past another set of bodies and found the wall on my left. Good, I could use it to guide my way to the corner. I gripped the cane, pulling its magic into myself.

Getting ready.

Bluish light filtered from beyond the next set of bodies, giving them a deeper hue of whitish blue. The air thickened with the stench of burned ash. I reached forward to the body on the left, ready to shove it out of the way.

The arm I grabbed felt like flesh.

I yanked my hand away.

My heart thundered in my ears. It couldn't possibly be a real body.

Could it?

No, another trick. Had to be. Every body in here was a prop. Just rubber. Cameron Rogers would never have a real body here.

I reached forward again. Grabbed the arm.

Rubber. Definitely.

I shoved it out of the way.

The girl was huddled in the corner, cowering from a dark figure in front of her. Terror was etched onto her face, heightening the white and blue makeup. Her mouth hung open in a silent scream. Tears started to flow down her cheeks, streaking the makeup. They were the only part of her that moved.

And the dark figure before her...

It was hard to fix my gaze on it. My eyes seemed to want to slide away, not to look. I blinked hard and tried again.

Same thing. My gaze wouldn't stay long enough to really see it. All I had was an impression of a dark figure.

I shook my head. No, I couldn't let it manipulate me. I couldn't let it hide. I had to see it.

I focused again, concentrating. Tightened my grip on the cane and drew from its power.

This time I could feel my gaze steady. Focus in front of the girl. There, yes, a dark figure wearing a long, hooded black robe. Thin, skeletal fingers with yellowed flesh stretched thin across the bones were pointed toward the girl, moving in precise movements.

Working a spell while it hid in the costume of a grim reaper.

Too clever.

"Hey, you wanna join the line and get some candy?" I yelled. I slammed the cane on the floor, sending a jolt of magic through, like a flash of heat through snow. It was an old spell, one I used to use at the North Pole to knock KJ off a snow pile when he was pelting me with snow balls.

It was enough of a jolt to distract the Phobophagus.

Enough to release the girl.

She collapsed, her hands hiding her face, smearing her makeup. The sound of her sobs mingled with the creepy music.

The Phobophagus growled.

It turned toward me, lifting its skeletal hands. The hood hung too far forward, creating deep shadows so I couldn't see the face within.

I didn't think I wanted to anyway.

"Found me, little Santa man," a deep, almost melodic voice came from inside the hood. "But you cheated. Wrecked my spell."

"I'll do more than that," I said. "You're finished here. Give it up."

Rumbling laughter peeled out, grating on my nerves.

"But I have only begun," the Phobophagus said. "The night is young and everyone wants to be scared. Perfect night for it. Perfect night for me."

"I'm on to you," I said. "The Council is on to you. We'll stop you."

"Will you?"

It breathed the words at me like a chilling wind with the stench of charred bones. My heart pounded in my chest. I fought to keep my breathing steady.

"If you're so confident why did you need that void spell?" My voice squeaked as I spoke. I cleared my throat and tried again. "You infected the home security system as a way to repel or capture any magic user that came near. But you couldn't help from being just a little bit flashy. Had to use the tombstones to send me a message."

A chuckle drifted out from beneath the hood. "Didn't want to make it too easy to enslave this world. Even I need a challenge."

The cocky arrogance in its voice made my heart pound again but this time with anger. A challenge? This had all been a game to this creature. Even Billy Blufield's death.

Game over.

"I've caught you now," I said.

"Caught me?" it said. "Found me, yes, because I allowed it. But caught me, not at all, little Santa man. I am the one who has caught you."

The skeletal hands shot out, reaching for me. I lunged backward, knocking the body to my right forward.

Right into the Phobophagus's clutches.

It snarled as it tangled with the rubber body. I darted to the left. Grabbed the girl's arm and yanked her to her feet. She stumbled as I dragged her forward.

Then she ran.

I shoved my way through the bodies, leaving them swaying behind us. The stench of ozone flooded the air. A build up of magic.

The Phobophagus was weaving a spell.

I couldn't stop it, it was too strong.

But I could try something else.

Through the swaying bodies, I caught a glimpse of the door. With a shove, I sent the girl stumbling in that direction. I darted to the left, lifting the cane.

I focused and mumbled the words of my spell. Remembering the last time I'd used it. Another time when I'd been fighting against KJ and a barrage of his snowballs.

When I'd made a snowman stumble toward him.

I swung my cane at the closest hanging body. It seemed to leap away as the wood contacted it.

In moments, all the bodies were swaying and struggling, rubber arms flailing.

A surprised roar sounded from the middle of the room.

Giving me enough time to dart toward the door and yank it open.

I leapt inside and slammed the door shut behind me.

With a tap of my cane, I forced the door to stick to the door jam.

Then I turned back to the room.

The silver metal morgue table was on my right. A plastic body with a large knife sticking up from the chest lay on top. Against the far wall, the girl in the smeared white makeup was sobbing in the arms of a tall, teenage boy who awkward patted her back. He wore a dirty lab coat and thick, black rubber gloves that went almost to his elbows. Makeup accentuated the lines in his face but still couldn't make him look older than twenty, not even with the grey splotches smeared into his hair.

From the shadows, a small figure stepped forward. Even under the distressed Elf hat, white curls poked out, looking soft and bouncy. The rest of the Elf outfit was a faded green with tattered cuffs and smudges of dirt on the black boots.

Venir's face twisted in concern.

"Is it?"

"It is," I said. "The Phobophagus. Get everyone out. Close the haunted house."

"Right, boss." The Elf turned away from me. At that moment, a couple entered from the other door, glancing around wide-eyed.

"Everybody out," Venir ordered. "The haunted house is closed." He glanced over at me. I shrugged. What excuse could he give? A magical Fear Eater wanted to terrorize them until they died from fright?

"Gas leak," the Elf said. "Everyone out."

The couple scurried back through the door. Venir pointed at the boy comforting the girl.

"You too. Out."

The boy shuffled toward the door, pulling the sobbing girl with him. With every step, the girl's sobs lessened, as if she realized she was moving farther away from the Phobophagus.

But it wasn't going to matter. The Phobophagus wasn't confined to the house. Once it realized no one else was coming through it would burst out onto the street to attack everyone.

Right how I wanted it.

Where we could contain it.

Where *I hoped* we could contain it.

The door behind me rattled. My quick spell to keep it shut wouldn't last long. I hurried after Venir through the other door. People crowded the end of the hall. Venir's authoritative shout pushed them all back. By the time we reached the front room, people were streaming back out the front door.

An actor sat in the rocking chair in the corner. Winter boots poked out from underneath the long, faded skirt. White hair, pulled back into a bun, looked slight askew on her head. The frown on her face added more years than the ghostly white makeup and dark lines.

"What's going on?" she asked. "People are supposed to be comin' in. Not goin' out this way."

"Problem in the house," I said. "We're shutting it down for a while."

"Mr. Rogers is gonna be pissed at this," she said.

"I work for him. It'll be fine." I gestured to the door. "That means you leave too."

She gave an exaggerated sigh and pushed herself up from the rocking chair. She took two steps toward the door when the sound of a crash echoed through the house, drowning out the ghostly moans and creepy music.

"What was that?" the girl asked.

"Out. Now."

I pushed her toward the door as a howling started behind us. A startled look flashed over her face. She darted away.

I followed.

As I slammed the door behind me and set another spell on the lock, I heard the grumbling of the crowd behind me. Then a familiar voice sounded.

"Noel, what's going on?"

Cameron stood behind me, arms crossed over his chest. Concern pinched his face, aging him.

"The thing that killed Billy is back," I said. "Move these people away from the haunted house. We'll take care of it."

Colour drained from Cameron's face. Without a word, he spun away from me. He raised his arms into the air.

"Everyone step back. The haunted house is closed. Please step back."

His voice carried over the laughter and rumble of people

talking. The laughter faded and the rumbling became more annoyed.

"Hey, I already paid to go through," said one man in a scuffed leather jacket.

"Are you really going to complain about five dollars when it goes to charity?" Cameron asked. With his arms crossed, he seemed to tower over the man even though the man had to be at least three inches taller. But the frustration and anger in Cameron's voice made the man wilt.

He shuffled back, mumbling under his breath.

Behind me, another crash sounded, closer this time. A bellowing roar filtered through the thin wood of the haunted house, making the walls shake.

Venir appeared at my side. A moment later, Palle stepped over the cemetery fence like it was a tiny garden fence rather than one that came up waist (on me) height. With swift movements, he moved to my other side. Talia hovered just above us, black wings blurred and almost invisible in the night sky.

I looked at them each in turn. They nodded to me once.

Ready.

As ready as we would ever be.

Time to face down the Phobophagus.

CHAPTER

TWENTY-ONE

Another crash sounded from the haunted house before us. Venir shifted uneasily. Somehow the undead Christmas Elf costume made him look younger, smaller, not his usual gruff and blustering self. I missed the blue jeans, the faded cowboy boots, and the t-shirts with inappropriate Santa Claus images on them.

He glanced over at me, a frown flickering at the edges of his lips.

"What if it throws the void at us?" he asked, bowing his head.

"There has been no time to perform the spell," Talia said. Her words floated down on us like cool rain. "It is complicated and time consuming. It has not had the chance to repeat it."

Relief eased some of the tension in the air. I could see

Venir almost sag with it. Then he straightened, squaring his shoulders.

I opened my mouth to speak but then the front door to the haunted house burst open.

The wood door slammed against the side of the house and hung askew, hinges broken. A dark figure filled the doorway, absorbing any light from behind it and before it.

Behind me, the crowd gasped. I heard footsteps and shuffling as they backed away. Voices rose in anxious murmurs but there was also curiosity. Did they imagine this was some kind of show that Cameron had put on?

I wished.

The figure floated forward, the edges shifting and flowing as it moved. By the time it reached the edge of the overhang, it had resumed the costume of the reaper again, complete with a silver scythe that rose above its head, the sharp point turned toward us.

With each step, the air filled with the scent of ozone, ashes, and charred bone. Over the murmur of the crowd, I could hear the Phobophagus chanting.

Casting a spell. Getting ready to sow fear and drink it in. Like some demented elixir.

I stepped forward and spread my arms. I took a deep breath and released it, sending out a wave of calmness, tinged with Christmas. The feeling of contentment after opening the presents and sitting down to share a meal with family and friends. The gratitude of having such splendid riches around you, regardless of the material items surrounding you.

I felt the peace spread through the crowd. The Phobophagus growled.

"You're fired from the haunted house," I shouted. My voice carried in the chill air. "Leave the premises immediately."

It had just occurred to me to pretend the Phobophagus was an actor. Maybe it was a way to keep the crowd's fear at bay.

A rumble sounded before me. It was the Phobophagus laughing at me.

"Foolish little Santa man," the deep voice crept across the sidewalk bringing icy dread. "Only brings me a larger meal."

The robes of the grim reaper costume rustled along the asphalt of the driveway as it stepped out from beneath the haunted house overhang. With each step, the figure seemed to grow, stretching taller until it towered over everyone.

Even Palle.

The murmurs from the crowd behind me changed from excitement to anxiety. Soon it would cross over into fear, exactly what the Phobophagus wanted.

Unless I did something to stop it.

If only I had an idea of what that something was.

I swallowed. My mouth tasted like ash. I glanced over at Venir. His face was whiter than the curls on his head. Palle had his teeth bared. His massive shoulders hunched, preparing for battle. Even above us Talia held her hands hooked into claws, ready to dive down to attack.

Wrong. This seemed all wrong.

A massive fight would be exactly what the Phobophagus wanted. Causing widespread panic and fear.

There had to be another way.

How could I stop it from scaring everyone? I'd never be able to sustain any Christmas magic during its onslaught. After all, it was Halloween. A time when people expected to be scared.

Of course. Halloween...

I tightened my grip on my cane and felt its magic trickle up my arm.

Time to fight fire with fire. Or in this case, fear with fear.

"You're fired," I repeated. "If you don't leave peacefully, we'll have to detain you." I lowered my voice. "For the Underwell."

The Phobophagus growled, lifting it scythe.

I swept my cane before me, chanting out a Christmas spell.

Venir jerked his head toward. Recognition flashed across his face. Then a grin lit him up. He started chanting along with me.

A special Christmas spell. One we used when testing out the dolls.

Whether they were battery-powered or just plain.

It was easier to have the dolls move themselves to test

their range of motion, rather than have each Elf perform the task by hand.

And when you had North Pole magic on your side....

Behind the Phobophagus, rubber bodies from the freezer room came bouncing out through front entrance to the haunted house. Many still had rope tied around the feet. A few of them had legs free. I flicked my hand, and set the ones with free legs doing high kicks. The others continued bopping up and down, arms flailing and flapping.

Venir's hand waved in front of him. The flailing arms steadied and began spelling out YMCA over and over again.

Laughter and cheers burst out behind us. The crowd began to applaud.

The Phobophagus roared. It swept its arms out. I could feel the crackle of ozone in the air as it gathered its magic.

Palle darted forward, head down as he charged.

Talia swooped in from the other side.

"Cameron," I shouted.

He ran to my side. I bent and whispered in his ear. He nodded and raced away, pushing through the crowd toward the side porch.

When I turned back, Palle had grabbed hold of the scythe and was trying to yank it away from the Phobophagus. The Phobophagus yanked back and they began a tug of war.

Talia darted forward and grabbed the hood of the reaper cloak. She yanked it down over the Phobophagus's hidden face.

The Phobophagus swatted at her, catching her on the leg. The smack sent Talia spinning away in the air.

The crowd gasped.

I drew the high-kicking rubber bodies closer to the Phobophagus. Several started kicking it from behind. The Phobophagus snarled, twisting to knock the rubber bodies away. Each one it touched dropped to the ground, like a marionette with its strings cut.

I chanted louder, focusing with the cane, but nothing I did affected those props. Whatever the Phobophagus had done had short-circuited my magic. I glanced over at Venir.

The Elf shook his head.

So much for those rubber bodies.

About ten were left, outside of the sweep of the Phobophagus's arm. As it twisted back to face front, Palle gave another yank. He roared with effort. Even in the yellow light from the streetlights, I could see sweat glisten on his green skin.

One final yank and he pulled the scythe from the Phobophagus's grasp. The Phobophagus swung at Palle with his other arm but the troll lurched back, dragging the scythe. The silver blade seemed to spark in the light but it could have been light glinting on the blade.

Venir darted forward to help Palle drag the scythe. The troll didn't even seem to notice the Elf. As Venir's hand closed on the handle, he jumped and with a yelp, let go.

He glanced back at me, his face pale. The scythe was definitely part of the Phobophagus's power and too strong for the Christmas Elf.

No wonder Palle was still struggling to drag it away.

The troll's massive muscles flexed and strained. Sweat glistened on his green skin. His lips were pulled back from his teeth, making the tusks on either side of his mouth seem longer and sharper. Palle had once told me they were mostly residual from a time when trolls gored their prey but were now non-functional, like an appendix. But the way they jutted from the troll face, I could imagine him running forward to ram into something with them.

Palle had managed to drag the scythe ten feet from the Phobophagus but that seemed as far as the Phobophagus was going to allow. With a growl, the Phobophagus stepped forward, following the troll. Another few steps and it would catch up.

Focusing on my intention, I slammed my cane down.

A blare of music burst forth from the front of the house. Two loud cords, one after the other. Then the beat started.

The crowd roared in approval. They raced toward the front of the house in a wave, abandoning the scene at the haunted house.

The Phobophagus paused. I was almost disappointed to not see the confusion on its face.

But of course it wouldn't recognize the music of Thriller.

The beat thrummed through the ground and then the vocals started. The crowd cheered and began to clap to the rhythm. I heard several singing along.

I stepped toward Palle. He steered himself in my direction, dragging the scythe. When he got close enough, I reached out and grabbed the pole.

A shock of power coursed through me. It was like grabbing a live electrical wire. The flood of magic felt like it was going to bowl me over. I could barely feel my other hand holding my cane or my feet on the ground. The magical wave was carrying me away...

Focus. My cane.

As I thought of it, I could feel it tingle, sending weak pulses up my arm. But it was enough to gather my attention. With effort, I thought of turning the wave toward my cane. It was like trying to redirect a tidal wave in my mind. The flood of it was too great for me to control. I could feel it slipping away from me. If I lost control, it would drag me under and probably burst out to kill every person here.

Fear chilled me. How as I going to do this? How could I direct this massive amount of energy?

I had to get it under control. It seemed an impossible task.

Then I felt the rumbling laughter in my mind.

The Phobophagus making fun of me.

Anger sparked within me. I was Noel Kringle, second son of Santa Claus. I wasn't going to let some two bit Fear Eater try to take down my client and my town.

So how was I going to control a tidal wave of magic?

I couldn't. But I could relate to a whirling blizzard of magic.

I focused on the image of a blizzard in my mind, all swirling snow and wind. Uncontrollable, and yet always with a purpose, a destination. An outlet.

I would give it that outlet.

I focused on the remaining rubber bodies and sent them bopping toward the cemetery display. At the same time, I focused on the other props inside the display. Boris the zombie. Karloff the vampire. All the others.

Time to give the folks a real show.

The music climaxed into the chorus and I let the props go.

The crowd roared approval as the rubber bodies and the vampire and zombies danced to Thriller.

I faced the Phobophagus.

"You've lost," I said. "You'll never scare them enough now. They'll think it's part of the show."

The Phobophagus snarled and lunged toward me.

I stumbled back, struggling to drag the scythe with me. It was like trying to pull a blizzard away.

From the corner of my eye, I saw Palle closing in from one side and Talia swooping in from the other. Both trying to attack the Phobophagus.

But it kept coming.

I stumbled another step backward. Then another.

The skeletal hand reached out.

Reached.

I clenched my jaw. Jerked back another step.

That hand...

It grabbed hold of the scythe.

Energy flashed through me. Everything went black. My body fell away and I was drifting in a black void.

The black void.

I felt myself panic but it was a distant, remote feeling. As it was happening to someone else. Heart pounding that felt like a soft thudding. Body struggling, almost like moving in water. Slow, languid.

All I had to do was relax. To let go.

No! That was what the Phobophagus wanted. Then it would take me.

Focus. Remember. I was here to stop the Phobophagus from feeding on the fear of Cameron's customers. To send it down to the Underwell.

We were both touching the scythe so the Phobophagus had to be here with me.

I concentrated. It had to be here. It had to be.

I felt a flicker.

Just a little.

It could be my imagination. Focus. Listen. Wait.

There it was again.

Not my imagination. It was the Phobophagus.

Right on the edge. Probably trying to gather enough strength to drown me in the void.

I knew what that was. I remembered losing myself. If I'd still felt my body, I knew it would be sweating, heart pounding in fear. I couldn't let that happen again. With the scythe and the Phobophagus here, I would never find my way out, even with the cane.

I had to stop it. But how? How could I fight fear itself?

No, it wasn't about fighting fear. The Phobophagus wasn't fear, it was a Fear Eater, subsiding on that emotion. It could cause the reaction through its use of magic but it wasn't fear itself.

Which meant that it could probably feel fear.

And what would a Fear Eater be afraid of?

Someone who would never be afraid.

I stopped struggling. The void stretched out around me, all black emptiness. I felt suspended within it, but no longer sinking. Not drowning.

I wouldn't drown because if the Phobophagus had the power to do it it would have already done it.

How much energy have you expended on this project?

I sent the words out around me. I felt them ripple like waves from a dropped pebble into a puddle.

Spreading outward.

The Phobophagus was not from this realm, so even maintaining its presence took energy. That was why it had latched onto a haunted house and cemetery display. It needed to piggyback onto the Halloween display to gather enough fear to feed itself. Without that, it wouldn't be able to get enough strength to attack.

Would it even survive I wondered. Maybe, but probably in some kind of low energy state, maybe something like hibernation. At the very least it would be powerless.

Unable to scare a fly.

Maybe this was its last blow out.

Here I thought it was some all powerful being when it was really some pathetic, low level creature that couldn't even protect its own spell in the haunted house.

How had I possibly ever been afraid of this joker?

Even this void wasn't really all that impressive. A good set of blackout drapes in my bedroom would create the same effect.

From a great distance, I could almost hear a growling. I could feel something tingling. After a moment, I felt it on what had to be my right side. In my hand.

The cane!

I could feel it, could feel my palm. I felt cool air between my lips. Smelled the rich odour of earth and vegetation, the scent of Cameron's yard that seemed to permeate the air for twenty feet around it.

Even the blackness of the void seemed less black, less cohesive.

Running on empty, aren't you?

A blast of anger ruffled through me like a hot breeze but I could feel something cold beneath it.

Fear.

The Phobophagus was afraid.

It had bet everything on its ability to generate terror at Cameron's house on Halloween but it had made a critical error. People expected to be scared at Halloween and they expected everything to be fake.

I laughed. I couldn't hear it but I could feel my throat vibrate.

At any other time, you would have created tremendous fear with your display of power. But no one believed it tonight. They don't even realize that the troll is real.

Another blast of anger enveloped me but this one was even weaker than the first. The Phobophagus was losing power faster now.

Think about it. How could you compete against vampires and zombies? You really miscalculated. No one here is afraid, not really. It's all for fun, the thrill of being scared without really being afraid because it's Halloween and everyone knows that fear on Halloween isn't really fear, it's fun.

The blackness of the void vanished, popping like a balloon. Light flooded my eyes, making them water. I blinked them away.

I could feel my body again. The air tasted sweet and chilly as I breathed in deeply. The cane in my hand seemed to quiver with energy. And in my other hand, the scythe felt like cold metal. The magic that had been pulsing through it was withering.

Like the creature before me.

The grim reaper cloak had shrunk lower, as if the being inhabiting it was shrinking. Fabric puddled on the ground. The skeletal hand still gripped the scythe. I yanked it back, breaking the hand's grip. It tried to reach for the scythe again, the fingers flexing weakly.

I stepped back, pulling the scythe with me.

The Phobophagus reached for it again, leaning forward. Leaning.

Then it fell. Breaking its fall with its hands.

Palle and Venir flanked me on either side. With a flutter of wings, Talia landed behind the Phobophagus. She tilted her head, studying the creature as it tried to crawl forward.

"Geez, boss, he's kinda pathetic," said Venir.

Talia lifted her gaze to me.

"You must have great magic," she said. "I cannot even detect it."

Venir snickered but stopped when I glared at him. Palle kept a bland expression on his face.

"I don't have great magic," I said. "In fact of all of us, I'm probably the weakest."

"Then how did you beat it?" Talia gestured at the Phobophagus.

"I stopped being afraid of it," I said. "We were feeding it ourselves. We'd built it up into this huge thing when it was really running on fumes. Think about it. Why had it created a spell to trap magic users?"

I glanced at each of them. Frowns and blank looks greeted me.

"It had to stop magic users because it knew it wouldn't be able to beat us in a fair fight," I said. "It made a big mistake coming here at Halloween. Yes, Halloween is about fear but that's the fun and no one believes it's real."

The music from the front yard finished with a flourish. A

roar went up from the crowd as they applauded. Soon they would be heading back this way, I knew.

"Talia, I think it's time to take the Phobophagus to the Underwell," I said. "Will you need help?"

A smirk lit up her face. "Not at all. I do not think I will even have a problem lifting it."

She darted forward, scooping her hands under the fabric. A mewling squeal came from within the cloak and she swept it into her arms. Her black wings spread open and began to flutter. In a moment, she was airborne.

She gave me a bow with her head.

"Thank you, Noel Kringle," she said. "I was wrong about you. The Council has made a good choice with you after all." She smiled. "Do not be surprised if you hear from them again."

Her wings flapped and she soared into the night sky. I felt a crackle of ozone and then a quick flash of light lit up the sky above the house.

Talia had slipped away into the Magical Realm.

"The Council?" Venir asked.

"Not now," I said. "Go tell Cameron to open the haunted house again. We've got a charity to raise money for. See if Shirl and Stan can tear themselves away from handing out candy to help us here. Palle, how do you feel about scaring people inside the house."

"Noel, it would be my pleasure," the troll said and gave me a smile.

With those tusks, I knew he would be a massive hit.

CHAPTER

TWENTY-TWO

The late morning sunlight had an anemic look as it poked through the clouds. I breathed in, tasting the scent of moist earth and sweet decay of leaves. Although it was after eleven in the morning, the air had a bite of chill as if teasing the winter to come.

I stood on the sidewalk with my hands stuffed into the pockets of my navy pea coat. I'd left my cane in the office as I knew I didn't need it anymore. In front of me, Cameron's front yard was already halfway through being packed up. First all the tombstones had been gathered up, then the lights, and now finally the props, including the multiple rubber bodies that had originally been inside the freezer room in the haunted house.

Palle, now wearing his regular human guise, stepped carefully over the grass until he reached the prop tucked into the bushes by the front walk. He reached in and lifted Boris the zombie out. Tucking it under his arm, Palle turned and headed back around the corner toward the garage.

The front door opened and Cameron Rogers stepped out. He carried two brightly coloured travel mugs. As he jogged down the stairs, the door swung closed behind him. He bounded down the front walk toward me then held out the bright pink travel mug when he reached my side. I noticed he kept the lime green one for himself.

"Coffee with a little splash," he said. His regular grin lit up his face.

I took the travel mug and sipped. Irish cream gave the strong coffee a real kick. It burned down my throat, making me gasp.

Cameron chuckled and took a sip of his own coffee. "Suzanne's only half way through counting the donations and we're already almost double last year," he said.

"That's wonderful," I said.

He nodded. "Yeah, I wish Billy had been around to be a part of it."

"Did Detective Mallory contact you?" I asked.

"Yes," Cameron said. "He mentioned that it was off the record but I appreciated him letting me know that they think it was an overdose." The sadness clouded his face again, then lifted a little.

"I've decided to make this year's donation in Billy's name," he said. "It won't bring him back but I hope it'll give some comfort to his family."

"That's a nice gesture," I said.

"That was a great idea of yours to put on Thriller when that guy started causing trouble," Cameron said. "Really distracted the crowd so you could take care of him."

I smiled and took a smaller sip. Warmth spread through my chest, taking the bite out of the morning chill.

"Folks seemed to enjoy the show," I said.

Cameron nodded, drinking his own coffee. Venir appeared at the end of the yard, leading Billy's two friends, Gavin Clifford, and Steve Kowalsky. The Elf's voice barked orders and his hand snapped out, pointing to several lights that had been left behind. The boys scurried to gather them up.

I stifled a grin. Venir was channelling his old supervisor persona.

Palle ambled by and Venir barked an order at him. The troll raised an eyebrow and kept walking, across the lawn. Venir glanced away, as if being ignored by the troll was exactly what he had planned.

"So are you going to open again next year?" I asked.

Cameron bowed his head to study the lid of his travel mug. The muscles on his forehead twitched as he thought. I waited, breathing in the soothing Irish Coffee scent over the earthy breeze that tugged at the edge of my coat like a puppy eager for attention.

"I guess I have to," Cameron finally said. "Seems kind of disrespectful not to, I mean with all these donations and all."

"I bet Gavin and Steve would like to help," I said.

"Yeah, might keep them out of trouble," he said.

The rumble of an engine sounded from behind me. I glanced over my shoulder. Mallory's sedan pulled up to the corner and stopped. He turned off the car and climbed out. The wind snapped at his beige trench coat but barely managed to ruffled his cropped brown hair.

As he stepped up to the sidewalk to join us, he gave a nod.

"Thought you might need some help with the tear down," he said. "But it looks like it's under control."

"We still have the haunted house," Cameron said. "I could definitely use another set of hands."

Mallory held out his hands, palms up. "Here they are."

"Great," Cameron said. "The guys are just finishing with the lawn and then we'll get started. Let me get you a cup of coffee."

He bounded up the front walk, heading for the door.

"How's he taking it?" Mallory asked.

"Like most people, he seems to have repressed the more unusual aspects of last night," I said.

Mallory snorted. "Unusual."

"Sometimes it's easier for people to ignore it," I said. "Even if that person loves Halloween." I tilted my head at him. "Did Billy really die of an overdose?"

Mallory shrugged under his trench coat. "It's possible. His friends did say he experimented with drugs. A toxicology screen from the autopsy will tell us for sure."

"But you don't have the results yet," I said.

"Nope."

"And you told Cameron anyway," I said.

"I told him off the record and that it was a strong possibility. With all the good he does for the Children's Healing Hospital, he doesn't need to think it was his fault, especially when it was some *thing* else entirely."

I could hear him emphasis on *thing*.

"Are *you* going to tell him differently?" he asked. "Or tell him how you got a bunch of static props and rubber bodies to do a dance to Thriller?"

"I'll tell him nothing," I said. "Halloween is a night of mystery and thrills. Why would he want to see behind the curtain?"

Mallory chuckled.

The front door opened as Cameron stepped through. He carried an extra travel mug.

Before I could warn Mallory about the Irish Cream in the coffee, Venir clapped his hands as he stood in the middle of the yard.

"All right you layabouts, you aren't here to watch the rest of us work," he snapped. "We got a haunted house to tear down. Move it!"

Gavin and Steve scurried across the lawn toward the driveway. Palle strolled after at his usual pace.

Venir marched forward a few steps before he stopped and spun to face Mallory and me.

"That means you too," he barked, his expression stern as he glared at us. Then he blinked and looked flustered.

"Ah, I mean, you too, boss. Please."

Mallory pressed his lips tight together but I could see them twitching out of the corner of my eye. I forced myself to look away so I wouldn't burst out laughing. I gave Venir a nod.

"We're on our way," I said.

I gave Mallory a nudge but he didn't move. Another nudge and still nothing. Finally, I elbowed him in the side. He gave a soft grunt.

"Okay," he said and started toward the corner.

"Before you get started, I've got your coffee," Cameron said as he hurried up. He handed a pale blue travel mug to Mallory.

Mallory took a healthy swig. His eyebrows shot up his forehead. He swallowed the gulp down.

"Good coffee," he said.

Cameron patted his arm and hurried along the sidewalk toward the haunted house.

"Nobody gives me coffee like this when I finish a case," Mallory said.

I smiled. "Maybe you should be a private detective," I said. "I could create an opening in my company."

Mallory snorted and laughed. "On second thought, never mind. I'll stick with regular old muggings, robberies, and murders. At least those make sense. Your cases, Noel." He shook his head. "Your cases are all so *weird.*"

I smiled and clapped my hand on his shoulder, steering him along the sidewalk.

"Stan," I said. "Weird is my specialty."

He opened his mouth to reply but Venir's sharp voice cut him off.

"Are you two gonna lollygag all day?"

"Coming, *boss*," I said.

The Elf blushed and turned away.

"Let's go tear down a haunted house," I said. "See? You never get to say that kind of thing in your regular police job."

"I never get sucked into a black void either," Mallory said.

I shrugged. "Every job has a down side."

This time, he did laugh which drew a sharp glare from Venir. We picked up our pace down the sidewalk.

Swirling snow, I did not want to incur any more ire from the ex-Christmas Elf about lollygaging around.

Although I had to wonder, what exactly *was* lollygaging?

I would have to remember to ask.

JOIN MY NEWSLETTER!

If you enjoyed this story, please consider taking a moment to review it or to recommend it to your friends. Reviews help other readers decide if a book is for them.

Sign up for my New Releases mailing list and get a free copy of the *Rebecca M. Senese Sampler*, featuring stories of science fiction, urban fantasy, mystery and horror. Enjoy them all!

Click here to get started: https://rebeccasenese.com/newsletter/

Santa's son is on the case

Enjoy more Noel Kringle with The Noel Kringle Chronicles!

REBECCA M. SENESE
Santa Claus:
PRIVATE DETECTIVE
THE NOEL KRINGLE CHRONICLES

REBECCA M. SENESE
SANTA MUST DIE!
THE NOEL KRINGLE CHRONICLES

REBECCA M. SENESE
THE CLAUS CONNECTION
THE NOEL KRINGLE CHRONICLES

REBECCA M. SENESE
THE TWELVE DEATHS OF CHRISTMAS
THE NOEL KRINGLE CHRONICLES

REBECCA M. SENESE
BABY, IT'S DEADLY OUTSIDE
THE NOEL KRINGLE CHRONICLES

REBECCA M. SENESE
THE MAN WHO WOULD BE SANTA
THE NOEL KRINGLE CHRONICLES

Acknowledgments

Special Thanks to all of the generous folks who sponsored me for the 2018 Muskoka Novel Marathon, benefiting the YMCA Literacy Services of Huntsville. I wrote the first 70 pages of this novel at the marathon and couldn't have done it without the generous support of these fine people.

Cathy Hope, Maura Dales, Evelyn Perdue, David Shtogryn, Paul Clinton, Victoria Wolf, Chris Ainsworth, Deb McGarvey, Julie Florio, CS, Lillian Parkinson, Gloria & Brian Williams, Ross Darlington, Sheri Wilkinson, Jason Hildebrandt, Juliana Tam, Louise Clare, Mandy Slater, Russell Martin, Gary Grisdale, Bob Clinton, Michael Darcy, Al Chiasson, Jennifer Kerr, Karen Mills, Laurie McEvoy, Heather Sinclair, Brenda Clark, Louise Hypher, and Jeff Fitzgerald.

ABOUT THE AUTHOR

Based in Toronto, Canada, I write horror, science fiction and mystery/crime, often all at once in the same story. I am the author of the contemporary fantasy series, the *Noel Kringle Chronicles* featuring the son of Santa Claus working as a private detective in Toronto. Garnering an Honorable Mention in *"The Year's Best Science Fiction"* and nominated for numerous Aurora Awards, my work has appeared in *Home for the Howlidays, Bitter Mountain Moonlight: A Cave Creek Anthology, Promise in the Gold: A Cave Creek Anthology, Unmasked: Tales of Risk and Revelation, Obsessions: An Anthology of Original Stories, Fiction River: Visions of the Apocalypse, Fiction River: Sparks, Fiction River: Recycled Pulp, Tesseracts 16: Parnassus Unbound, Ride the Moon, Tesseracts 15: A Case of Quite Curious Tales, TransVersions, Deadbolt Magazine, On Spec, The Vampire's Crypt, Storyteller, Reflection's Edge, Future Syndicate* and *Into the Darkness*, amongst others.

Find me online:
www.RebeccaSenese.com

www.NoelKringleChronicles.com
www.RebeccaSeneseBooks.com

facebook.com/Rebecca.M.Senese

bsky.app/profile/RebeccaSenese.com

x.com/RebeccaSenese

bookbub.com/authors/rebecca-m-senese

instagram.com/rebeccamsenese

goodreads.com/rebecca_senese

wandering.shop/@rebeccasenese

www.ingramcontent.com/pod-product-compliance
Lightning Source LLC
Chambersburg PA
CBHW032026180726
48283CB00008B/2833